CALL AND RESPONSE

THE STORY OF BLACK LIVES MATTER

CALL AND

THE STORY OF

RESPONSE

BLACK LIVES MATTER

BY **VERONICA CHAMBERS** WITH **JENNIFER HARLAN**

VERSIFY

Houghton Mifflin Harcourt · Boston · New York

Versify® is an imprint of Houghton Mifflin Harcourt Publishing Company. Versify is a registered trademark of Houghton Mifflin Harcourt Publishing Company.

hmhbooks.com

Photo credits can be found on page 147.

The text was set in Granjon LT.

Cover design by Whitney Leader-Picone and Samira Iravani

Interior design by Monique Sterling

The Library of Congress Cataloging-in-Publication Data is available.

ISBN: 978-0-358-57341-8

Manufactured in Canada

Friesens 10 9 8 7 6 5 4 3 2 1

4500826852

Front cover text from Frederick Douglass, Diane Nash, Malcolm X, Janelle Monáe, Melina Abdullah, Alicia Garza, John Eligon, Somini Sengupta, Colin Kaepernick, Nikkolas Smith, DeRay Mckesson, James Weldon Johnson, Menace Two and Resa Piece, and John Lewis

Back cover photos (clockwise from top right):
June 6, 2020, in Washington, DC (Michael A. McCoy for The New York Times); June 8, 2020, in New York (Demetrius Freeman for The New York Times); June 7, 2020, in New York (Gabriela Bhaskar for The New York Times); June 9, 2020, in New York (Simbarashe Cha for The New York Times); June 14, 2020, in New York (Simbarashe Cha for The New York Times); Oct. 3, 2020, in Seattle (Paul Christian Gordon/Alamy)

Lead author
Veronica Chambers

Coauthor
Jennifer Harlan

Photo editor
Anika Burgess

Editing support
Brian Gallagher

Research
Nick Donofrio

Art production
Steve Brown, David Braun, William O'Donnell, Sonny Figueroa

Caption support
Lauren Messman

Original reporting, editing, and production for "Who's Who at a Protest"
Juliana Kim, Simbarashe Cha, Lily Benson, Meghan Louttit, Andrew Hinderaker

Editorial director for Book Development
Caroline Que

Special Projects editor
Monica Drake

We'd like to dedicate this book to the teachers and librarians who inspired us to become readers and journalists. In particular, we'd like to thank Arthur and Louise Hillman, Pat Sharpe, Dana Thompson, John Herzfeld, Marti Calderwood, and the librarians of the Rugby branch of the Brooklyn Public Library.

A Black Lives Matter march in Brooklyn on Juneteenth in 2020. The holiday, celebrated on June 19, marks the day in 1865 when the last enslaved Black people in the United States were told that they had been released from bondage by the Emancipation Proclamation.

CONTENTS

Black Lives Matter demonstrators at a march in Manhattan on June 4, 2020.

INTRODUCTION

A TRANSFORMATIVE SUMMER

A young Black man, looking not much older than eighteen or nineteen, stands in the dark of night. The moon casts a glow around his face. Dozens of police officers in riot gear—helmets, body armor, wielding batons—stand just a few feet away from him. The lights from police helicopters shine down like spotlights on a stage.

He's protesting the death of another Black man, one who was killed by the police. With his back straight and his eyes focused, he faces a sea of uncertainty. He doesn't know the faces behind the helmets. More importantly, he can't read the minds of those holding the weapons. He doesn't know what they might do—in an instant—if they deem him a danger.

He has come to a protest. He has taken a leap, going from just a feeling he might have had in the privacy of his home to a public statement, made in the streets. The man stands in the dark, but he is not alone. He is part of a movement—one that gives him greater power than he could ever have alone.

All around him, filling his neighborhood and others like it across the country, are hundreds of thousands of Americans who also feel compelled to take a stand. They are of all ages, races, and faiths, hailing from all walks of life. But they have come together in a common cause. They have heard the same call, and when they respond, they speak in one voice: a chorus that demands to be heard.

"Whose streets?"

"Our streets!"

In the spring and summer of 2020, the streets of the world, and especially of the United States, were filled with this call and response by people demanding change. This explosion of activism came out of a protest movement that had been building for years, since the summer of 2013. It started with three women who had been thinking about the issues of race, justice, and equality since childhood. And the spark that would set the whole thing off was a simple statement, first expressed by one of them in a Facebook post: *"Black lives matter."*

Protesters in the Black Lives Matter movement joined a long line of activists and advocates for racial justice in America. That legacy stretches back to the earliest days of the nation's history, through generations of people who have worked to make the country more equitable. At a pivotal moment, some people seemed to wake up to a reality many of their fellow citizens had recognized for years: that the deaths of Black Americans at the hands of police or vigilantes were not isolated tragedies, but the results of a

system shaped by racism and all its resulting injustices.

So they stood up. They marched. And they chanted the names of those who had recently been lost. Ahmaud Arbery, twenty-five, a former high school football star who was shot and killed while jogging in February by two white men in Georgia who chased him down in a pickup truck. Breonna Taylor, twenty-six, an emergency room technician who was shot and killed in her home in Kentucky in March by a white officer during a botched police raid. George Floyd, forty-six, a hip-hop artist, security guard, and father who died in Minnesota in May after a white police officer handcuffed him and knelt on his neck for more than eight minutes.

The Black Lives Matter protests hit their peak in the United States on June 6, 2020, when close to half a million people rallied in 550 locations across the nation on a single day. Experts believe that between fifteen million

and twenty-six million people participated in some type of Black Lives Matter event throughout the spring of that year—most likely making it the largest protest movement in the nation's history. And the movement did not stop at America's borders.

In London, hundreds of people flooded Trafalgar Square.

In Berlin, multiracial crowds held signs that read WE NEED JUSTICE. JUSTICE CAN'T WAIT.

In Paris, protesters dressed in black held signs that said, I CAN'T BREATHE, WE ARE ALL GEORGE FLOYD, and RACISM CHOKES.

In Idlib, Syria, two artists drew George Floyd's brown eyes and chiseled jaw amid spray-painted stars on a cinder block wall that reached up into the sky.

In Brisbane, Australia, thousands of people flooded the downtown streets, many of them wrapped in the country's Aboriginal flag, which honors its indigenous people.

In Nairobi, Kenya, dozens of people were arrested as they protested incidents of police brutality that occurred both abroad and in their own neighborhoods. LIFE IS PRICELESS, the marchers' signs declared. SAVE OUR FUTURE.

In Bangkok, protesters unable to gather in person because of the coronavirus pandemic shared photos and videos of themselves standing up for Black Lives matter and held a moment of silence on Zoom in honor of Floyd.

All across Canada—from Vancouver to Toronto—thousands marched. One protester held a sign that read WHO DO YOU CALL WHEN COPS MURDER??? Another held a sign that quoted the Reverend Dr. Martin Luther King Jr.: INJUSTICE ANYWHERE IS A THREAT TO JUSTICE EVERYWHERE.

The women who started it all—Alicia Garza, Patrisse Cullors, and Opal Tometi—were moved by the way Black Lives Matter had spread, but they were not surprised. "One

In the late spring and summer of 2020, protests spread to every corner of the United States–from Minneapolis, where George Floyd was killed, to the nation's capital and coast to coast from New York to Portland, Oregon.

Black Lives Matter protesters in Dakar, Senegal, on June 6, 2020.

thing I'm very clear about is that there's so much we have in common," Garza told *Vanity Fair* in 2020. "We all want to live lives where we feel safe, where we are able to live with dignity, and where we're connected."

So how did we get to this point, where the whole world seemed to rise to its feet to condemn racism and injustice? Why were the people compelled to march? How does a moment grow into a movement? What it comes down to is a truth that Garza, Cullors, and Tometi, as well as those who joined them and those who came before, knew well: the power of the people is greater than the people in power. And when the people stand together, they can change the world.

Two young artists, Anna Barber and Connor Wright, created this memorial in Minneapolis to victims of police brutality, crafting plastic headstones for George Floyd and other Black people who had been killed. They started with one hundred names and added more based on submissions from community members, many of whom also came to light candles and lay flowers before the gravestones. A marker at the front of the installation, which the artists titled *Say Their Names Cemetery,* read: "How many have there been? How many more must there be?"

THIS IS WHAT PROTEST LOOKS LIKE

What do we mean when we talk about protest? Yes, it's people gathering in the streets. It's walking for miles, chanting call-and-response slogans that share a vision for change. It's taking a knee. But it's also making art with a message. It's leaving flowers at a memorial. It's writing emails and calling elected officials. It's making brownies for a bake sale and donating the proceeds to a cause you believe in.

In the spring and summer of 2020, people across the United States found many different ways to take a stand for Black Lives Matter. In New York, a protest organized by the collective Street Riders NYC drew more than a thousand bicyclists. Ringing their bells, the cyclists called out "Whose streets? Our streets!" as they rode from the Barclays Center arena in Brooklyn to Manhattan's Central Park.

In Havre, Montana, a Black college student named Dorian Miles joined more than one hundred people at a Black Lives Matter rally. Miles had never felt at ease in Havre, which is 81 percent white—until the protest. "For the first time, in three months since I've been here, I felt safe," he told the *Havre Daily News*. "I felt like the city I moved to gave me a hug."

In Washington, DC, the pastry chefs Willa Pelini, Paola Velez, and Rob Rubba created Bakers Against Racism, a virtual bake sale to raise money for Black Lives Matter. People around the world signed up to make and sell desserts of their choosing and donated their proceeds to local BLM chapters and other organizations fighting for racial justice. They raised more than $2 million in seven months. "Everybody has a role to play," Pelini told *Washingtonian* magazine. "And you can use what you're good at to push forward the cause."

Each of the millions of people who participated in the protests of 2020 was moved to take that stand by something different—something personal. For the legendary civil rights leader John Lewis, it was when he was fifteen years old and first heard Martin Luther King speaking on the radio. "We may not have chosen the time," Lewis later said. "But the time has chosen us."

These marchers outside the Barclays Center arena in Brooklyn on June 5, 2020, were among the millions of people who stood up and demanded justice for George Floyd.

In the weeks and months that followed Floyd's killing, demonstrations spread to more than 150 cities across the country—including Ferguson, Missouri, which had been the site of previous uprisings against police brutality and racism. These protesters knelt in front of a police line in Ferguson on May 31, 2020.

Although Floyd's death was the spark that ignited the 2020 protests, it was compounded by two other tragedies: the shootings of Ahmaud Arbery in February and of Breonna Taylor in March. This makeshift memorial for Taylor was erected in Jefferson Square Park in Louisville, Kentucky, where daily protests over her killing continued for months.

In the late spring and early summer of 2020, Black Lives Matter demonstrations spread to big cities—like New York, pictured here on May 31—small towns, and everywhere in between. "Really, it's hard to overstate the scale of this movement," Deva Woodly, an associate professor of politics at the New School, told *The New York Times* in July.

All told, at least fifteen million Americans participated in some sort of Black Lives Matter action in 2020, likely making it the largest protest movement in the country's history. This man marching in Harlem was part of the crowd that flooded the streets on June 4, chanting, "Say his name! George Floyd!"

K'Marie Dixon participated in a "peace ride" for racial justice, organized on June 7, 2020, by the Compton Cowboys. Riders chanted "No justice, no peace" as they guided their horses through the California city, accompanied by hundreds of marchers on foot. "I never imagined anything like this," Randy Hook, one of the cowboys, told *The New York Times.* "We're making our family proud, our 'hood proud, and our city proud."

The Black Lives Matter movement started in the wake of the death of seventeen-year-old Trayvon Martin, who was killed by a neighborhood watch volunteer in Florida in 2012. It has been driven, throughout its history, by the tragic loss of Black lives and by a demand for justice, expressed on this sign at a march in Brooklyn on June 6, 2020.

"WHOSE STREETS?"

Protesters in 2020 flooded the streets on foot, by skateboard, on bicycles, and in roller skates. This demonstration in New York on June 27 drew more than a thousand cyclists. "It's like riding in the cavalry," Paige Acevedo, twenty-nine, told *The New York Times*.

Black Lives Matter started as a movement to end gun violence and police brutality, but it quickly expanded to confront a host of issues resulting from systemic racism, which has shaped the United States since its beginning. Supporters of the movement, like these protesters in Washington, DC, on June 3, joined the lineage of Americans who have fought for racial justice and civil rights.

"OUR STREETS!"

George Floyd's final words resonated with Americans who felt suffocated by a centuries-old system of racist oppression. The rallying cry "I can't breathe" moved millions of people, like this protester in New York on June 4, to stand up and demand change. But Black Lives Matter didn't start as a mass movement. It started with three friends, a Facebook post, and a moment of grief, outrage, and determination that would echo around the world.

From left, the Black Lives Matter cofounders Opal Tometi, Patrisse Cullors, and Alicia Garza accepting a Glamour Women of the Year Award in 2016. "They channeled our collective anger, frustration, grief, and determination into action," the producer Shonda Rhimes said when presenting the trio with the honor. "And in doing so, these women have fundamentally altered the course of civil rights in America."

CHAPTER 1

THREE GIRLS WHO WANTED TO MAKE THE WORLD BETTER

Today, Black Lives Matter is a global movement that has rallied millions of people to the cause of ending racial injustice and police brutality. But it began as a conversation among three women: Alicia Garza, Opal Tometi, and Patrisse Cullors. The trio did not plan to start a mass protest movement. They started out as three young girls who cared deeply about their communities and about doing their part to make those communities safer, more just, and more equitable for all.

Alicia Garza was twelve years old when she became an activist. She grew up in Northern California, the daughter of a Black mother and a white stepfather, both of whom were antiques dealers. Garza and her family stood out in their town of Tiburon. Of its nearly nine thousand residents, fewer than one hundred were Black, and Garza was one of only ten Black students, out of about three hundred, at her middle school. When her school district became embroiled in a debate about reproductive rights and sex education for middle-school students, Garza stepped into the fray. Campaigning on the side of more education and access to birth control for teens, she convinced the schools to make contraception available to students and to offer comprehensive sex ed. The experience of speaking out for what she believed in and seeing her classmates respond positively to her leadership was empowering. "That spurred me to really want to be an asset to my community and to make sure the people I knew and loved had all the tools they needed to make the decisions that were right for them," she told *Vanity Fair* in 2020. "It also spurred me to want to do more."

As a social sciences student at the University of

From an early age, Alicia Garza was committed to community service and activism. "Ever since I was young, I've had this notion that people should be able to live their full dreams," she told *Vanity Fair* in 2020, "not when everybody else is asleep, but while they're fully awake."

California San Diego, Garza continued advocating for access to birth control, for HIV/AIDS testing, and against domestic violence. U.C.S.D. was also where she started to study politics and began to organize communities as she figured out how she wanted to spend her time and energy as an adult. "It was far enough from home where I felt like my parents couldn't just drop in on me unexpectedly, but it was close enough that if I needed my mom's home cooking, I could get home within a day and get a hug and a good meal," Garza recalled.

After college, she got an internship at the School of Unity and Liberation (SOUL), an Oakland training program for social justice organizers. People study and train to be activists just as they would to become firefighters or paramedics. She began working for Just Cause Oakland, an advocacy group that successfully fought for eviction protections for low-income tenants in the area. She spent the summer learning how to canvass—knocking on doors and talking to more than a thousand residents about the work Just Cause was doing and the resources that were available to them. "I spent countless hours in kitchens and living rooms, on crowded couches and porches, and in backyards," she writes in her book, *The Purpose of Power: How We Come Together When We Fall Apart*. "I learned how to engage other people in the slow process of changing the world." It was also where she met her future husband, Malachi Garza, a transgender man and fellow organizer.

Alicia was twenty-three when she told her parents that she was queer. "I think it helped that my parents are an interracial couple," she said in an interview with *The New Yorker*. "Even if they didn't fully understand what it meant, they were supportive."

She started working as an organizer for more community groups, including People United for a Better Life in Oakland (PUEBLO), the UC Student Association, and People Organized to Win Employment Rights (POWER). At POWER, she led the outreach initiative to the Black community, fighting for both racial and environmental justice. Over the next decade she continued working in Oakland, speaking out against police brutality and fighting for free public transportation for young people.

Opal Tometi, another of Black Lives Matter's co-founders, followed a different path to activism. Tometi grew up in Arizona, witnessing the ongoing conflict over immigration on the border between the United States and Mexico.

The immigration issues came even closer to home when Tometi's parents, who are Nigerian immigrants, faced possible deportation for being undocumented. They were able to secure the right to stay in the United States, but others in their community were not as fortunate. When Tometi was in high school, her best friend's mother was deported, so she moved in with Tometi and her family for a while. The threat of deportation and how it echoed through her community made Tometi passionate about

immigrant rights. She would later tell *The Guardian,* "It instilled in me just how vulnerable [my family was] to the whims of the state."

Tometi attended the University of Arizona, and in 2004, while taking a class on the Holocaust, she drew parallels between the history she was studying and the perils facing the immigrant community where she grew up. She recalled telling her classmates, "'Look around us, y'all. Look at what we're saying about immigrants, the way we're talking about people being "illegal," look at the types of laws being pushed . . .' I remember everybody, especially my instructor, just shutting me down."

That experience stuck with her into her adult life, when she decided to focus her attention on the rights of

For Opal Tometi, Black Lives Matter was always so much bigger than one individual name or tragic loss. "What was important was that we were living in a society where, systematically, our loved ones could be taken from us," she told *The Guardian* in 2020. "And there would be no justice."

> ## "ME BEING THE DAUGHTER OF IMMIGRANTS, ALICIA AND PATRISSE BEING QUEER; NATURALLY OUR OWN IDENTITIES INFORM THE WORK."
>
> —Opal Tometi

immigrants and their families—families like hers. She eventually became the executive director of the Black Alliance for Just Immigration, an organization in the Bay Area, where she helped reunite families after the earthquake in Haiti in 2010 and advocated for Black immigrants before the U.S. Congress and at the United Nations.

Patrisse Cullors, the third cofounder of Black Lives Matter, grew up in the San Fernando Valley in Los Angeles, an area of great income inequality.

The daughter of a single mother and a father who was in and out of prison, Cullors remembered her childhood as being shaped by poverty. Her mother struggled to make a living, and the closing of the local General Motors plant had a disastrous effect on the family's income. In her book, *When They Call You a Terrorist: A Black Lives Matter Memoir,* Cullors writes about how she and her siblings ate Cheerios with water because they couldn't afford milk, and how the family lived without a working refrigerator for more than a year. "Being hungry is the hardest thing, and to this day I have prayers of gratitude for the Black Panthers, who made Breakfast for Children a thing that schools should do," she recalls. "We qualified for free lunch and breakfast, and without them I am almost sure we wouldn't have made it out of childhood alive despite my hardworking parents."

As she grew up, she became increasingly aware of her own sexuality. She came out as bisexual when she was in tenth grade. Her cousin Naomi, who was already out, was the first person she told. Toward the end of her junior year, Carla, one of Cullors's best friends, was kicked out of her home, and the two of them spent their last year or so of high school staying on friends' couches or living in Carla's car. After graduation, their art history teacher offered them a more permanent place to crash. Cullors lived with her for nearly two years. "Donna Hill, a simple, single Black woman with a heart that could carry a universe, becomes my first spirit guide, the first and most clear example I have as a young adult of what it means to receive a gift you can only properly show gratitude for by sharing it with others," she writes in her book.

Hill told Cullors about the Brotherhood Sisterhood social justice camp—a training program for young organizers. "Campers are like me: poor, Queer, and Black. But they are also heterosexual. They are working and middle class and some are quite wealthy. They are Latinx. They are white," Cullors recalls in her memoir. "The goal is to train a generation to be in conversation with one another and we confront all manner of difference and all manner of discrimination . . . We have highly facilitated, cross-racial dialogues

that allow us to be wholly honest about the stereotypes we hold about each other." This kind of training would prepare her to work within organizations that examine bias and promote equality, and to take that activism to the streets.

As part of the camp, several social justice organizations came to make presentations to the budding activists and talk about their work. Cullors was drawn to one of them in particular: the Labor Community Strategy Center, which uses a combination of grassroots organizing, policy development, education, and art to advocate for working-class communities of color.

After the camp ended, Cullors spent a year training with the Center as an organizer, focusing on engagement with young people. She read lots of books, studying political philosophy and feminist theory. She produced spoken-word events to reach young people in the community. And she canvassed for a group that was working to improve access to public transportation for low-income riders. Her training at the Center set her up for a career of engaging in social justice work to help families and communities like hers. In

It was important to Patrisse Cullors that Black Lives Matter be actively intersectional and make space for those who had been overlooked in past campaigns for social change. "We have centered and amplified the voices of those not only made most vulnerable but most unheard, even as they are on the front lines at every hour and in every space: Black women—*all* Black women," she writes in her memoir, *When They Call You a Terrorist.*

2012, she founded Dignity and Power Now, a grassroots organization in Los Angeles that advocates for incarcerated people, their families, and their communities.

Like Garza and Tometi, Cullors was actively involved in the struggle for justice and the empowerment of people of color. And it was this work that brought the women together. Her path first crossed with Garza's at an event during a political conference in 2005. As Garza described it, the pair "became fast friends on a dance floor in Providence, Rhode Island."

In early 2013, Cullors recalled, a Black leadership network called BOLD, Black Organizing for Leadership and Dignity, brought all three of the women together. They bonded over their love for their communities and their passion for using their voices to make a difference.

These women came to activism with different backgrounds and specific interests, but they all saw the bigger picture and the ways in which their causes were connected. And when it came to Black Lives Matter, the scope of the movement—the ways that police brutality intersected with other issues—was apparent to all three of them. As Tometi told *The Guardian* in 2020, "From the beginning, when I built BlackLivesMatter.com, I went to the website and wrote: 'Black queer lives matter, Black immigrants matter, Black disabled folks matter . . .' This movement is about all of us and recognizing that Black people aren't a monolith."

She noted that embracing the complexity of the issues began with each founder owning her story. "Me being the daughter of immigrants, Alicia and Patrisse being queer; naturally our own identities inform the work," she said. And by bringing their full selves to the work of organizing, they served as role models for younger organizers. "These women were my first real glimpse of the power of Black queer women," Thandiwe Abdullah, who was nine when Black Lives Matter started, wrote in an essay for *Refinery29*. "They helped me begin to decolonize and unlearn everything I thought I knew about what it meant to identify as she/her. They taught me pronouns, they taught me gender fluidity, and all of the intricacies of blackness."

When the summer of 2013 rolled around, all three of the founders were in their late twenties or early thirties and doing the slow work of grassroots organizing: knocking on doors, building relationships with people in their communities, and working with local residents to enact change. United by a desire to work for racial equity and better living conditions for all Americans, they had committed, from an early age, to doing that work in their neighborhoods and cities. And soon, they would be engaged in something much bigger: a national movement that eventually spread around the world.

A Black Lives Matter demonstration in Times Square on June 7, 2020.

Demonstrators in New York on July 14, 2013, protest the acquittal of George Zimmerman in the death of Trayvon Martin.

CHAPTER 2

IT STARTED WITH A LOVE LETTER

On February 26, 2012, Trayvon Martin, a Black seventeen-year-old from Florida, was walking home from a convenience store after going out for a late-night snack run. Dressed in a hoodie, he was carrying a pack of Skittles and a can of AriZona watermelon juice cocktail when George Zimmerman, a neighborhood watch volunteer, confronted him. Zimmerman shot Martin in the chest, killing him.

Zimmerman claimed that he killed Martin in self-defense, invoking Florida's "stand-your-ground" law. He talked about how the teenager was dressed and the fact that Martin was Black. In the media, many pundits defended Zimmerman. On Fox News, Bill O'Reilly declared, "It's a bit complicated because the reason Trayvon Martin died was because he looked a certain way and it wasn't based on skin color . . . But he was wearing a hoodie and he looked a certain way. And that way is how 'gangstas' look."

Alicia Garza was appalled by this reasoning: "The conversation that was happening in the media was, 'What did Trayvon do to cause his own death?'"

For many, Martin's killing was a heartbreaking reminder of the reality facing their own brothers, nephews, and friends. Barack Obama, the nation's first Black president, shared words of sympathy for the family and called for a thorough investigation into Martin's death. "If I had a son, he'd look like Trayvon," he said.

Garza, Patrisse Cullors, and Opal Tometi all had brothers who looked like Trayvon. And his killing hit home for them. "My brother is six feet tall and has a huge Afro, and I thought, That could have been my family," Garza recalled in 2015. "I remember thinking about my fourteen-year-old brother and literally not being able to sleep," Tometi said in an interview.

For Cullors, Martin's everyday errand that suddenly ended in his death reminded her of the fear she felt walking around her own neighborhood in Los Angeles, where she grew up witnessing what she called "state violence." "I remember the police officer who would patrol our block and who would harass my siblings," she said. "And I remember feeling frightened most of the time."

Garza was sitting in a bar in Oakland with her husband and friends on July 13, 2013, when the verdict in the Zimmerman case was announced. When the jury found him not guilty, the room went silent, she recalled in an interview with *The California Sunday Magazine*. At first, everyone was stunned, then furious. *How could this have happened? How could the jury not believe a crime had taken place when an unarmed teenager had been shot to death?* But pretty quickly, the shock and outrage gave way to jaded acceptance. "What I was seeing on social media were a lot of statements about 'We knew he was never going to be convicted of killing a Black child,' and 'What did you expect?'" she said.

It was this acceptance of what so many Americans—of all backgrounds—agreed was a breach of justice that moved Garza the most.

"When it was announced that the jury had acquitted George Zimmerman of all charges, it actually felt like I got punched in the gut," Garza recalled in another interview. "So I went on social media to try to find words for what was happening, and what I wanted in that moment was some love for us. And so I wrote a love letter to Black people on Facebook."

In a series of posts, Garza poured out all her frustration and fear and heartbreak. *"Our lives are hanging in the balance,"* she wrote. *"Young black boys in this country are not safe. Black men in this country are not safe."* At 7:19 p.m. she posted what would become the spark that ignited a movement:

"BLACK PEOPLE. I LOVE YOU. I LOVE US. OUR LIVES MATTER."

Protesters of all ages gathered in New York's Union Square on July 14, 2013, for a rally protesting the acquittal of George Zimmerman. The demonstration swelled to thousands of people and brought traffic to a standstill as the crowd marched to Times Square.

Cullors was visiting a mentee—a Black eighteen-year-old named Richie who was serving a decade in Soledad State Prison for robbery—when the verdict came through that night. She and Garza texted each other, sharing their shock and pain. When she saw Garza's post, Cullors shared it, adding #blacklivesmatter.

Within days, the hashtag began spreading online. The Dream Defenders, a group that protested against the stand-your-ground laws that were used to justify shootings such as Martin's, occupied the state capitol of Florida. A week after the verdict, more than a thousand protesters marched across the Brooklyn Bridge. The Design Action Collective reached out to Garza, and she worked with them and Cullors to create a Black Lives Matter logo.

Tometi took things to the next level. As Garza would later tell it, Tometi reached out to her and said, "I saw what you wrote on Facebook the other day. It resonated with me. It's resonating with a lot of people. What if we take this energy that's online—everybody talking, posting memes and pictures—what if we take that energy and create platforms for people who want to fight back against anti-Black racism, against state-sanctioned violence in all of its forms? What if we created a space for people to come together who want to fight back, so that they could do more than like and share and retweet, but that they could actually do things together offline?"

Tometi took Cullors's hashtag and created a Facebook page, a website, a Tumblr page, and accounts on Twitter and Instagram. The idea, Garza explained, was to create ways for Black people to organize that would be welcoming to all voices. "That's how Black Lives Matter was born," she said. "We utilized our networks, people who we're connected to across the country and across the world. And that idea and those platforms were accessible to everyone, regardless of where you were, how much money you made: everybody could be a part of that conversation."

As Alicia wrote on Facebook just three days after that first post:

"#BlackLivesMatter is a collective affirmation and embracing of the resistance and resilience of Black people . . . It is a rallying cry. It is a prayer . . . #BlackLivesMatter asserts the truth of Black life that collective action builds collective power for collective transformation."

For the next year, Garza, Cullors, and Tometi used the Black Lives Matter hashtag to mark and share cases where they saw racial inequality resulting in death and other tragedies, at the same time creating an online community centered on the struggle to end police brutality. "If our goal is to change the culture, to even get people to believe in and speak the words Black Lives Matter, that first year is one of fits and starts," Cullors recalls in her memoir. "We are able to talk about the horrifics as they roll out with regularity. We hashtag names again and again."

Garza, Cullors, and Tometi believed deeply that an antiracist movement would make life in the United States better not just for Black people but for *all* people. And from the beginning, they saw the movement's campaign against police violence as deeply connected to other issues, too, including women's rights, workers' rights, and the need to build Black political power. "What unites them for me is that everyone right now is longing for something different,

Alicia Garza's words became a rallying cry for those outraged at the killing of Trayvon Martin and at the deaths of thousands of other Black people like him whose lives were cut short.

something better," Garza said in a 2020 interview with *National Geographic*. "In the midst of all of the grief and rage and pain, there's a hopefulness. There is a longing for who we can be together. This movement crosses so many others, which shows that we can build new kinds of communities where everybody can belong, and where everyone can be valued and where everybody can be powerful. And that is what drives me to be a part of these movements. It's what motivates me."

The protesters vowed to continue fighting for justice not only for Trayvon Martin but for all Black people. "There's a new level of energy," the Reverend Markel Hutchins, who helped organize a protest in Atlanta, told *The New York Times* in 2013. "There's a new level of enthusiasm that I personally have not seen since the days of the civil rights movement. Perhaps Trayvon Martin's death–and perhaps even the not guilty verdict in the George Zimmerman trial–has inspired and ignited a movement of people who, frankly, needed to be moved."

Protesters and law enforcement face off during a "Weekend of Resistance" in October 2014–part of the months-long protests in Ferguson, Missouri, in the wake of the killing of Michael Brown.

CHAPTER 3

A MOMENT BECOMES A MOVEMENT

On August 9, 2014, in Ferguson, Missouri, nineteen-year-old Emanuel Freeman was at home getting ready for work when he heard a gunshot. He looked out his window and saw a white police officer, Darren Wilson, shooting a Black kid in the street. Then the kid, eighteen-year-old Michael Brown, fell to the ground.

Freeman went to Twitter and posted:

I JUST SAW SOMEONE DIE. OMFG.

Brown's body was left on the street, under the blazing sun, for nearly four and a half hours. People passing by saw and stopped. They told their neighbors. They shared it on social media. By evening, word had spread throughout the community.

Brown had just graduated from high school and was days away from starting his freshman year at Vatterott College. His killing came just a few weeks after a Black man named Eric Garner had died in Staten Island, New York, after Daniel Pantaleo, a white police officer who was arresting him for selling "loosies"—single, untaxed cigarettes—placed him in a chokehold. Cell phone videos captured Garner's last words: "I can't breathe. I can't breathe." The grief and outrage in the wake of these deaths would mobilize thousands of people, giving rise to public demonstrations across the nation.

In Ferguson, protests began the night after Brown was shot and continued for weeks. People came from all over the country to take part. Some of them were trained organizers who had experience rallying their communities. Others had never been to a protest before. All of them made this moment a turning point. Their work focused the nation's attention on police violence and racial injustices, and it turned Black Lives Matter from a growing but small conversation on social media into a rallying cry that was heard around the world.

Johnetta Elzie, then twenty-five, had grown up in St. Louis. Her mom had recently died, and one of her best friends—Stephon Averyhart, a young Black man like Brown—had been shot and killed by police earlier that year. She had spent months in a haze of despair and grief. "I was depressed from January to July," she said in an interview for this book. "In August, I pulled myself together because my sister was about to be a freshman in high school. She had no mother, so her big sister had to get her shit together. Then, literally as I'm like, okay, I'm dedicating my life to being a big sister and showing up for her and doing what Momma would want us to do, Mike is killed."

When Elzie heard about Brown's death, she went to the apartment complex near where he had been shot. A crowd had started to gather. Johnetta—or Netta, as she is called by friends—had studied journalism at Southeast Missouri State University. She began posting online what she saw. *"It took them 4 hours to even put a sheet over the baby's body. Had him laid there bleeding out from 10 gunshot wounds. For 4 hours,"* she tweeted.

From her first posts about the Brown incident, Elzie

"All I had was my Twitter and my Facebook and my Tumblr and Instagram," Johnetta Elzie told *The New York Times* in 2015. "And so I just felt, and I really believed, that someone somewhere would care about what I was seeing."

became one of the movement's most powerful chroniclers and leaders. (She noted, in an interview for *Complex* magazine, that although she is often called a Black Lives Matter activist, she aligns herself with what she simply calls "The Movement.") She and other people in Ferguson used Twitter, Facebook, Instagram, and other social media platforms to share an unfiltered look at what was happening in their community and to draw attention to the protests even before the media started to focus on the story. In an interview with *Teen Vogue,* Elzie described her role as "documentation and getting the actual news from the perspective of the citizens." As she told the magazine, "I think the media was attracted to my voice because I counteracted the news and I was just raw and honest."

Around the globe, as people shared, liked, and commented on her posts and those of others, a worldwide awareness grew of what was going down in Missouri.

The day after Brown's death, a memorial and peaceful candlelight vigil was held for him in Ferguson. Thousands of people from the community showed up to mourn, filling the streets as some of them chanted, "No justice, no peace!" The police sent in hundreds of officers in riot gear, armed with rifles and K-9 units, to control the crowds. Officers, captured on camera, wouldn't allow people to gather publicly. They said: "If you are in the middle of the street, you are unlawfully assembled. Disperse immediately."

Many of the protesters were upset by what they viewed as a militaristic response to a moment of deep grief. The gathering took a turn. Some protesters set a gas station and convenience store on fire. They smashed windows and overturned several cars. The police responded by tear-gassing the crowds, shooting them with rubber bullets, and arresting those who gathered. Images of Ferguson dominated news websites, quickly spread on social media, and were broadcast live on TV. The fear, frustration, and outrage over a long-standing pattern of police brutality would keep Ferguson in turmoil for weeks to come. "I would not even call it a protest," Elzie recalled. "Those first weeks were military occupation."

Images of the uprising in Ferguson, and the police response, spread across social media. "I think they thought this would just go away," one protester, Katherine Fenerson, told *The Guardian* in October 2014. "I think it's surprised them we've been so resilient." Months later, on the first anniversary of Michael Brown's death, the demonstrations continued.

A protester runs through a cloud of tear gas in Ferguson on August 17, 2014. The law enforcement response to the demonstrations—where officers often showed up with tactical gear, body armor, and armored vehicles—sparked criticism of the militarization of American police. "At a time when we must seek to rebuild trust between law enforcement and the local community," Attorney General Eric Holder said, "I am deeply concerned that the deployment of military equipment and vehicles sends a conflicting message."

Just a few miles away, in St. Louis, a twenty-nine-year-old woman named Brittany Packnett heard the news of Michael Brown's death. A former elementary school teacher, Packnett was the executive director of the St. Louis branch of Teach for America. Her parents, a minister and an educator, had been longtime leaders in the city's Black community. "My dad was an activist, and mom has always been in community leadership," she told the journalist Wesley Lowery, who covered the protests for *The Washington Post*. "So, truth be told, my first protest was probably while I was still in a stroller."

Packnett, who now goes by Brittany Packnett Cunningham, was already a leader in her community and stepped forward as a key voice during the protests. She was appointed by Missouri governor Jay Nixon to serve on the Ferguson Commission, a group of sixteen leaders who represented "a diversity of communities, experiences, and opinions." They were charged with conducting a "thorough, wide-ranging and unflinching study of the social and economic conditions that impede progress, equality and safety in the St. Louis region."

For Packnett Cunningham, the fight was personal. As she later told *NPR*, "I'm a North County kid," referring to the area of Missouri where Ferguson is located. "These are my people. Mike could have been my brother."

DeRay Mckesson watched the Ferguson protests on television from his home in Minneapolis. Like Packnett Cunningham, he'd been a teacher with Teach for America. At the time of the protests, he was working for the local school district.

On impulse, he got in his car and drove nine hours to Missouri. He would later say that his goal was to "bear witness." At the time, he wasn't a huge force on social media; he had roughly nine hundred followers. But he tweeted his ride to Ferguson.

After he was tear-gassed on one of the first nights he

Brittany Packnett Cunningham–seen speaking at a Martin Luther King Day service at Atlanta's Ebenezer Baptist Church in 2019–was part of a cohort of young, Black activist leaders that emerged during the Ferguson protests.

joined the protests, his tweets went from commentary on the cost of gas and bad drivers to the kind of citizen journalism that became a cornerstone of the Black Lives Matter movement.

He tweeted, *"Y'all, tons of police."*

And: *"Tear gas. It has begun #Ferguson."*

A little while later: *"Also, the noise sirens are out. Tear gas feels like extreme peppermint tingling. F.Y.I. #Ferguson."*

Thirty tweets later he sent one more: *"Phone is dying. I am nowhere near my car. I am lost in #Ferguson. Really bad car accident. Looting across from it. Pray for me. #Ferguson."*

"I just couldn't believe that the police would fire tear gas into what had been a peaceful protest," Mckesson told *The New York Times Magazine* in 2015. "I was running around, face burning, and nothing I saw looked like America to me."

Mckesson was frustrated by much of the media coverage of Ferguson, which often placed the blame for violence at the protests on demonstrators rather than police. The majority of protests in Ferguson were peaceful, and as they stretched on for weeks, they became more and more organized, with local groups coordinating rallies, marches, and acts of civil disobedience. But in the media, the focus remained on the largely isolated incidents of looting or vandalism, and the narrative of the Ferguson uprising as a violent riot persisted. "Organized protests—unlike the half dozen or so nights of rioting—almost never resulted in violence, except for tear gas from responding officers," journalist Wesley Lowery explains in his book, *They Can't Kill Us All: The Story of the Struggle for Black Lives.* "The momentum seemed to keep growing in the streets, spurred on, in part, by the simple truth that police kept killing people."

A couple of weeks into the protests, at a medic training in Ferguson on how to respond to tear gas, Mckesson met Elzie, who shared his frustration. Together with Packnett Cunningham and a law professor named Justin Hansford, they started the *Ferguson Protester Newsletter*.

"NOTHING I SAW LOOKED LIKE AMERICA TO ME."

— DeRay Mckesson

"Mckesson and Elzie decided together that instead of letting the media control the narrative, they would curate media content—circulating the pieces that got it right and calling out the outlets that got it wrong," Lowery writes in his book. Among the newsletter's "most powerful features was the day counter near the top of each edition:

"# of days since Darren Wilson has remained free: 50

# of apologies from the Mayor of Ferguson: 0

# of protesters arrested last night: 24"

The newsletter, which was distributed via email and later came to be known as *This Is the Movement,* grew to more than twenty thousand subscribers in a matter of months, "keeping the protests in the headlines and near the front of the nation's collective consciousness during the months between Michael Brown's death and the grand jury decision—a crucial three-month period when a diversion of the nation's attention could have forever muted the growing movement," Lowery writes.

Black Lives Matter was one of the first U.S. social movements to successfully use the internet as a mass mobilization device. It built on the work of such international movements as the Arab Spring in 2011, in which young activists in North Africa and the Middle East used social media to organize their campaigns to topple despotic regimes across the region. In the United States, Frank Leon Roberts, a professor at New York University who specializes in contemporary social movements, writes, "BLM will forever be remembered as the movement responsible for popularizing what has now become an indispensable tool in 21st-century organizing efforts: the phenomenon that scholars refer to as 'mediated mobilization.'" Social scientists use this term to describe campaigns for change that use social media to rally people for collective action. While previous social justice movements had to rely on word of mouth, flyers, or community groups to tell their stories and then wait for word to gradually spread throughout the media about their cause, social media enabled the Black Lives Matter activists to share and shape their own narrative. Tweets like Mckesson's and Elzie's put a vast network of people in the protesters' shoes and made the events on the ground visceral and real, even for people who were hundreds or thousands of miles away from Missouri. With hashtags like #blacklivesmatter and #ferguson, those who couldn't participate in the protests physically could still join in the movement—online, from wherever they were in the world, as one united force.

The speed with which the protesters were able to spread the word about what was happening in Ferguson was a marked change from previous movements for racial justice. There was no such thing as social media on April 12, 1963, when Martin Luther King was arrested for demonstrating without a permit during an antisegregation protest in Birmingham, Alabama. From jail, he wrote a letter to his fellow clergymen, in particular to white people who had called his push to end segregation "unwise and untimely." King powerfully described the work of civil rights activists as patriotic and entirely aligned with the ideals of the founding fathers. "We will reach the goal of freedom in Birmingham and all over the nation, because the goal of America is freedom," he wrote.

It took months for those powerful words to be heard by a national audience. By the time *The Atlantic* published King's letter in its August issue, under the headline "The Negro Is Your Brother," King was long out of jail. (Later

In his "Letter from a Birmingham Jail," Martin Luther King argued for protest as a powerful tool for making urgently needed change. "We know through painful experience that freedom is never voluntarily given by the oppressor," he wrote. "It must be demanded by the oppressed."

that month, he would lead the March on Washington and give his famous "I Have a Dream" speech.) But Americans of all backgrounds were moved by his words. Many now call the "Letter from a Birmingham Jail" the most important document of the civil rights movement.

King's letter was rooted in the principle of love as the motivating force for change. He had studied the work of the Indian activist Mahatma Gandhi, who in the early twentieth century led his nation's fight for independence from Great Britain in a campaign that was centered on civil disobedience, a form of political protest in which activists refuse to comply with rules or laws that are unjust—such as restrictions on where people of a certain race are allowed to sit on a bus—in order to demonstrate the unfairness of the policies. Gandhi's philosophy of Satyagraha, a "truth force" or "love force," called for activists to hold themselves to a higher order of truth and love. Gandhi strongly advocated peaceful protest and believed that "in a gentle way, you can shake the world."

The year after King wrote his letter, Nelson Mandela, another advocate of civil disobedience, was arrested for protesting apartheid, a system of racial segregation that kept Black South Africans oppressed for almost fifty years. Mandela spent twenty-seven years in prison, but he never wavered in his conviction that racist practices and beliefs could be overcome. In his autobiography *Long Walk to Freedom,* Mandela wrote, "No one is born hating another person because of the color of his skin, or his background, or his religion. People must learn to hate, and if they can learn to hate, they can be taught to love, for love comes more naturally to the human heart than its opposite."

King studied Gandhi's words and work carefully, and he spoke of love—not as a romantic ideal, but as a powerful force to sway hearts and minds—constantly as he marched, wrote, and organized. "Love is the only force capable of transforming an enemy into a friend," he said.

These principles of radical, peaceful protest and civil disobedience became the hallmarks of the civil rights movement in the United States. In 1961, for example, the Congress of Racial Equality (CORE) organized a group of activists to ride buses into the South to protest the segregation of buses and bus terminals, which the Supreme Court had recently ruled was unconstitutional. CORE's proposal was simple: a multiracial group of riders, white and Black, would travel by bus from Washington, DC, to New Orleans. If anyone tried to remove the Black riders or make them use separate facilities along the way, they would refuse. The protests became known as Freedom Rides.

Thirteen activists—men and women of various ages and from different parts of the country—were selected for the first ride: among them was a twenty-one-year-old organizer from Alabama named John Lewis, who would go on to become a renowned U.S. congressman. The riders spent a couple of days training in Washington, role-playing different scenarios and practicing how to respond nonviolently to the abuse they expected to endure on their journey. On May 4, the crew boarded two buses to start their trips. And, as anticipated, they faced violent opposition along the way. In towns across the South, the buses were met by angry mobs who attacked the riders with pipes, baseball bats, and bicycle chains. At a stop in Alabama, thugs firebombed one of the buses and held the doors shut to try to keep the Freedom Riders from escaping. When they did manage to get out, the mob attacked and beat them. Many of the activists were arrested and thrown in jail. Lewis himself

More than three hundred Freedom Riders were arrested in the summer of 1961. Top row (l. to r.): John Lewis, twenty-one; Margaret Leonard, nineteen; Kredelle Petway, twenty; Hezekiah Watkins, thirteen; Ernest Newell Weber, fifty-two. Middle row: the Reverend C. T. Vivian, thirty-six; Stokely Carmichael, nineteen; Marilyn Eisenberg, eighteen; Rita Carter, eighteen; Joan Trumpauer, nineteen. Bottom row: Catherine Burks, twenty-one; Albert Earl Lassiter, nineteen; Helen O'Neal McCray, twenty; the Reverend Grant Harland Muse, thirty-five; Shirley Smith, forty-three.

spent a month in a Mississippi prison and was beaten several times. After one attack in Montgomery, Alabama, he was left lying unconscious outside the Greyhound bus terminal in a pool of his own blood.

But no matter what kind of violence or opposition they were met with, the Freedom Riders didn't retaliate, and they didn't back down. CORE organized more than sixty Freedom Rides during the next several months, involving more than four hundred riders. And ultimately they were successful. President John F. Kennedy, bowing to pressure from these young activists, directed the Interstate Commerce Commission to issue new rules enforcing the desegregation of all interstate buses, terminals, and other facilities.

Half a century later, the protesters in Ferguson looked to their predecessors as models for how to successfully and nonviolently campaign for change. Inspired by the work of Lewis and others, Patrisse Cullors and Darnell L. Moore, a writer and activist from New Jersey, organized a series of Black Lives Matter Freedom Rides to Ferguson. In August 2014, five hundred activists traveled to Missouri as part of the demonstration. Their varied backgrounds included community organizing, law, public policy, media, and the arts. They all came together to support the protests and to strategize for a line of sustained action that would continue well after the crowds eventually dispersed.

Melina Abdullah, a professor of Pan-African studies at Cal State Los Angeles and cofounder of the Los Angeles chapter of Black Lives Matter, was one of the activists who took part in the Freedom Rides. She and her daughter Thandiwe were part of a group that drove across the country from California in five large passenger vans; at age ten, Thandiwe was the youngest participant, and the oldest volunteer was a man in his eighties. "In our van, we had both ends of the spectrum and everything in between," Melina recalled in an interview for this book.

Before they left, the organizers decorated the vans, covering them with the painted names of Black people who had been killed by police and with slogans including "Black Lives Matter." "We didn't really take into account the fact that we were driving across the country in places that were a lot more conservative than L.A.," Thandiwe said. In some areas, people rolled down their windows to yell at them and hurl racial slurs and insults at the caravan. Eventually the group pulled into a gas station in Texas for a bathroom break, and some of the organizers suggested that, for their own safety, they wash the paint off. But Thandiwe disagreed.

"I was ten," Thandiwe, now seventeen, recalled, "and I was like, I don't think we should do that." When the adults asked what she meant, she said, "The whole point of this ride is that it's supposed to make people aware of what's going on, to make people confront this reality of what we experience every day." The group agreed to keep the paint, all the way to Missouri.

For Thandiwe, it was a formative moment, teaching her the value of speaking up. "BLM has never been a space where youth voices have been silenced," she said. "Everything that any of us said was always taken into account just as much as anyone else." (She and her younger sister, Amara, would go on to found the Black Lives Matter Youth Vanguard, fighting to get police out of public schools in Los Angeles.)

The protests over Michael Brown's death spread to more than 150 cities. In New York, Justice League NYC—an initiative of The Gathering for Justice, a social justice organization founded in 2005 by the singer and veteran civil rights activist Harry Belafonte—helped organize demonstrations across the city that brought traffic on the Brooklyn Bridge to a halt and shut down the West Side Highway in Manhattan. Belafonte was joined in this work by Carmen Perez, a former parole officer who started Justice League and would go on to help organize the 2017 Women's March—a massive demonstration for gender equality and justice that drew millions to protests in Washington, DC, and around the world on the day after the inauguration of President Donald Trump.

The events in Ferguson also marked the moment when the Black Lives Matter movement started to go global. As the historian Barbara Ransby writes in her book *Making All Black Lives Matter*: "Media from all over the world showed up to cover the Ferguson story. Palestinians halfway around the world watched the uprising on television, followed it through social media, and tweeted statements of solidarity. Banners shared on social media and held up by solidarity delegations that eventually visited Ferguson read, 'Palestine Stands in Solidarity with Ferguson' and 'Ferguson to Palestine: Occupation Is a Crime.'" Activists from the other side of the globe shared practical advice with the Ferguson protesters about how they could protect themselves from tear gas. And in countries like South Africa, organizers held their own events that "linked the injustices faced by Black people on that continent with the struggles of the people of Ferguson," Ransby writes.

Black Lives Matter became the subject of sermons and began to take hold even in groups whose primary focus wasn't racial equality. Medical professionals rallied to support the group under the banner of White Coats for Black Lives. The Center for Constitutional Rights formed Law for Black Lives, which eventually became a standalone organization.

It was a transformative moment for the emerging movement. "#blacklivesmatter would not be recognized worldwide if it weren't for the folks in St. Louis and Ferguson who put their bodies on the line day in and day out and who continue to show up for Black lives," Cullors wrote in 2016. "And yet, we knew there was something specific about Ferguson and the efforts of the brave organizers in Ferguson that made this moment different: more radically intersectional, more attuned to the technology of our times, more in your face."

Alicia Garza would end up spending almost a month in Ferguson helping local organizers plan what became known as a Weekend of Resistance. In that time, she felt a shift from trying to get residents to join specific events to engaging them in a movement that would continue long after a single protest or rally.

Old-guard civil rights leaders like the Reverend Al Sharpton and the Reverend Jesse Jackson also came to Ferguson to join the fight, but they were not embraced as readily by the young protesters already on the ground. Both Sharpton and Jackson saw the Black church as a central engine for social change, as it had been during previous generations' fights for racial justice. But when Jackson showed up in Missouri and used a speech at a rally to ask for donations to his church, it was seen as a thoughtless insult in a community where so many of the residents lived below the poverty line. The protesters booed him off the stage.

An even deeper cause of the rejection of these older leaders was that Jackson and others subscribed to a philosophy that the Harvard University professor Evelyn Brooks Higginbotham calls the "politics of respectability." They believed that by speaking, dressing, and acting a certain way, they could prove to the people in power—namely, white people—that Black people were honorable and deserving of the respect and human rights they had been denied for so long in this country.

The activists of Black Lives Matter saw things differently. They appreciated the value of the nonviolent tactics that had accomplished so much during the modern civil rights movement, but they also embraced the radical self-determination of the Black Power movement, which had grown out of the movement led by King and others. The BLM activists believed that Black people didn't need to prove they were worthy of equality and justice. Being human entitled them to those rights.

If Black Lives Matter began after the killing of Trayvon Martin with a love letter and a hashtag, it was from Ferguson and the aftermath of Michael Brown's killing that a generation of young activists emerged—finding friendship, strength, a common goal, and the first glimpse of how powerful they could be when they stood up, marched, and shared on social media what they saw and heard.

In the spring of 2016, DeRay Mckesson–seen here canvassing–ran for mayor in his hometown of Baltimore, which had recently been roiled by protests over the death of a Black man, Freddie Gray, in police custody. He finished sixth in the city's Democratic primary.

Mckesson would later write that it was in Ferguson where he confronted his deepest fears, and that he found the courage to choose the path of activism. "I learned hope the hard way," he wrote in *The Guardian*. "Hope is the precursor to strategy. It powers our vision of how to bring about a desired goal, and it amplifies our efforts. I am not surrendering to luck, or a blind faith that things will just get better. I am reminded that to have faith that a world of equity and justice will emerge does not relinquish one's role in helping it do so. This is the way to use hope: as faith's companion, and vice versa."

Some of the young leaders who emerged from Ferguson, like Elzie and Mckesson, were moved to action by the moment. Others, like Packnett Cunningham, approached the moment of tragedy with years of experience working in organizations that were focused on social justice. Each in their own way believed that Ferguson was the beginning of facing America's deep racial inequality in a powerful new way.

"This was the start of a new civil rights movement in America," John Eligon, a reporter who covered the events in Ferguson for *The New York Times,* explains. "It started with efforts to right the criminal justice system that disproportionately targets Black and brown people. But then the agenda expanded to include more things: segregated schools and housing, investment in Black communities and businesses, political power."

Black Lives Matter picked up a baton that had been passed from generation to generation of Americans working, often through protest, for racial justice. As Mckesson would later write: "We did not invent resistance or discover injustice in August 2014. We exist in a legacy of struggle, a legacy rooted in hope. But hope is not magic. Hope is work. Let's get to the work."

Attorney General Loretta Lynch, Brittany Packnett Cunningham, President Barack Obama, and Representative John Lewis meeting at the White House in 2016.

CHAPTER 4

SO MANY WAYS TO BE AN ACTIVIST

After Ferguson, some activists looked to Alicia Garza, Opal Tometi, and Patrisse Cullors to lead the Black Lives Matter movement. But that had never been the women's goal. As Black Lives Matter groups began popping up in communities across the country, the cofounders created the Black Lives Matter Network to centralize the organizing principles of the movement, and they hired staffers to handle communications and coordination among the chapters. But they urged each of those groups, which soon grew to eighteen, to work independently on the campaigns and issues they found most pressing in their own communities.

In December 2014, a new coalition formed, called the Movement for Black Lives. It included the Black Lives Matter group, now called the Black Lives Matter Global Network, as well as organizations such as Dream Defenders, the multiracial group that had occupied the Florida capitol after the killing of Trayvon Martin and which was now focused on defunding the police and rebuilding communities, and the Million Hoodies Movement for Justice, an organization—now known as Brighter Days for Justice—working to combat gun violence and mass incarceration.

In July 2015, more than fifteen hundred associated members of the Movement for Black Lives gathered at Cleveland State University to discuss the expanding platform that had begun growing out of the initial movement against police violence. This included issues such as food justice in Black neighborhoods, Black feminism, equal rights for Black members of the LGBTQIA+ community, and reparations for slavery. "There was no doubt what this weekend was about: the defense of black bodies, the celebration of black collective resiliency, and the building of a movement the likes of which has never been seen," Mark Winston Griffith, a community organizer from Brooklyn who attended the gathering, wrote in *The Nation*. In response to the rallying cry of #BlackLivesMatter, Griffith said, "a new generation of black change agents has emerged—people who are organizing youth, queer, and transgender folks, women, immigrants, the differently abled, and other black communities." And the convention, he wrote, was "the first significant attempt to bring these organizers under one roof."

Later that month, Garza helped organize another conference in upstate New York called "Now That We Got Love, What Are We Gonna Do." It was a sort of Black Lives Matter strategic planning meeting. The attendees gathered movement-building tactics from veteran civil rights leaders like Bob Moses, scholars such as Barbara Ransby, and long-time activists like Makani Themba. The idea was that the next time they were called to action by a tragedy or injustice, the young activists would be prepared to seize the moment.

As Black Lives Matter grew, its young leaders followed multiple paths. Some concentrated on protests and organizing within their communities. Others created formal organizations and focused on working toward policy changes, often with lawmakers on the local, state,

or national level. In other words, some worked inside the existing political system while others worked outside of it—a strategic choice that had faced the activists who came before them.

In 1962, Dolores Huerta, along with Cesar Chavez, formed the National Farm Workers Association (NFWA), an organization that worked tirelessly to improve the lives of migrant workers and first-generation Americans who worked on the farms that provided our nation's food. Huerta coined their slogan *"Sí se Puede"*—or "Yes, We Can." (Four decades later, that phrase would find another life as a slogan during Barack Obama's 2008 campaign for president.)

While Chavez focused on organizing at the community level—often through such nonviolent protests as pickets, boycotts, or strikes that targeted specific farms that were exploiting their workers—Huerta focused on policy change, lobbying on behalf of all farmworkers for more equitable laws. She knew that for their movement to be successful, they needed both kinds of leaders. More than half a century later, she is inspired by Black Lives Matter and what these young activists have accomplished in a relatively short time. "This is the reason I, at the age of 90, continue to work," she told *The New York Times* in 2020. "When people come together and take collective action, whether it's in a march, whether it's in a union election or, most important,

In 1965, Dolores Huerta and the NFWA helped organize a five-year, nationwide consumer grape boycott that led to better pay, benefits, and safety protections for thousands of farmworkers.

come together to vote, this is how we make change. In the women's suffrage movement, they marched and marched. Marching and protesting are important. But I like to say

to people who are protesting and marching that until you put something into a law that can be implemented, that can be enforced and where people can be held accountable, we have to keep on marching right to the ballot box."

The Reverend Leah Daughtry faced a similar choice when deciding how to enter public life. Her father, the Reverend Herbert Daughtry, was a pastor and community activist who worked with leaders both domestically and internationally, including Jesse Jackson and Nelson Mandela, so she grew up around organizers who were deeply engaged in fighting for justice.

In her book, *For Colored Girls Who Have Considered Politics,* Daughtry recalls how her father showed her that there were two paths to making lasting change: "My father always stressed the importance of having people who were your *inside* men and women, who worked within the traditional structures of government and the white-majority seats of power, and the *outside* people who worked with and on behalf of the people first and foremost." Like Huerta, Daughtry ultimately chose to become an inside woman: she is now one of the highest-ranking Black women in Democratic Party politics, having served as chief of staff for the Democratic National Committee, as the chief executive of the 2008 and 2016 Democratic National Convention committees, and as as an advisor to Vice President Kamala

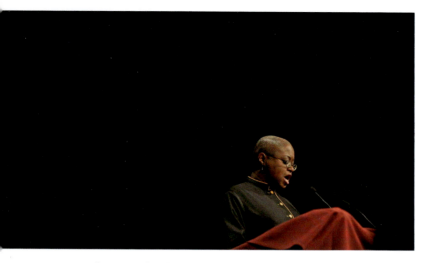

The Reverend Leah Daughtry speaking at an interfaith gathering of religious leaders before the 2008 Democratic National Convention.

Harris. And she has used her position to push for equity and justice for Black people, particularly Black women.

This inside-versus-outside question confronted the young people moved by Black Lives Matter as the movement grew in scope. After Ferguson, DeRay Mckesson left his job and decided to devote his life full-time to organizing. "It was one of those moments where I was like, I am willing to do whatever it takes to make sure that nobody else has to deal with this ever again," he said in an interview for this book. He defaulted on his student loans, used up his retirement savings, and bounced around between friends' basements and spare rooms. "I really didn't have it figured out," he recalled. "But I knew that what I was doing was right and what the police were doing was wrong. And I was willing to let that truth be it."

Ultimately, he chose a mostly inside path. He decided to run for mayor of Baltimore and, along with his friends and fellow activists Johnetta Elzie and Brittany Packnett Cunningham, as well as Samuel Sinyangwe, an organizer and data scientist, he cofounded Campaign Zero, a policy-based organization dedicated to ending police brutality in America. Elzie also helped start the database Mapping Police Violence, which tracks killings involving law enforcement personnel across the United States, and the advocacy group We the Protesters, which provides resources and tool kits for organizers. She rejected attempts to categorize the work she did under a single label. "I don't even really call myself an activist, that's something people say to describe what I do," she told *Jezebel* in 2015. "I was doing what everyone should be doing if you say that you love where you're from and your people. I was born and raised in St. Louis and I love everything about growing up here. It just so happens that Black people get killed by the police often here and I was tired of it."

Mckesson saw the value in both types of work. "We can actually change the world if we implement changes on the inside," he said in the 2016 documentary *Stay Woke: The Black Lives Matter Movement*. "But also, people need to press from the outside. Pressing from the outside forces things that would otherwise not happen. We need both."

Meanwhile, Brittany Packnett Cunningham went right to the heart of political power itself. On December 18, 2014, just months after the killing of Michael Brown, President Barack Obama signed an executive order creating the President's Task Force on 21st Century Policing. At thirty, Packnett Cunningham was one of the committee's youngest members. Obama reportedly told her that she was a "voice who is going to make a difference for years to come." In her, Black Lives Matter, just three years after its inception, had an inside woman with a seat at one of the most powerful tables in the nation.

The young leaders of Black Lives Matter worked in different ways, but they were united in their goal of fixing a legal system that to them was clearly broken, particularly when it came to law enforcement. The task they set for themselves was made particularly difficult by just how major a force the police are in America. There are some eighteen thousand law enforcement agencies in the United States, including local, state, and federal police forces. The United States currently spends more per capita on policing than almost any other country in the world. In 1960, that number was roughly $17.8 billion a year, adjusted for inflation. By 2018, it had ballooned to $137 billion. And yet, in that same amount of time, the reported crime rate rose from about 1,887 crimes per 100,000 Americans to 2,580 crimes per 100,000, and the number of violent crimes went from 161 in 1960 to 381 in 2018.

In 2020, one of the most consistent chants heard at Black Lives Matter protests was "Defund the police!" But what does this mean exactly? Alex S. Vitale, a Brooklyn College professor and the author of the book *The End of Policing,* writes, "I'm certainly not talking about any kind of scenario where tomorrow someone just flips the switch and there are no police." Vitale and other reformers argue that one primary cause of the problems with law enforcement today is that the police are given too many tasks that other agencies

A demonstrator outside a Chicago police station on July 24, 2020, holds a sign calling for the defunding of the police, which became a popular rallying cry at that summer's protests.

could handle in a better way, and that shifting funds to these other departments would actually make communities safer. Police today are expected to do much more than solve and prevent crimes. They are asked to manage car accidents and domestic disputes and truancy, to address calls that relate to people who are dealing with serious mental health challenges or addiction. When someone's dog is missing, the first call is often to the local police.

Some police officers agree that it's too much. In 2016, David Brown, then the chief of police in Dallas, put it this way: "We're asking cops to do too much in this country . . . Every societal failure, we put it off on the cops to solve. Not enough mental health funding, let the cops handle it . . . Here in Dallas, we got a loose dog problem. Let's have the cops chase loose dogs. Schools fail, give it to the cops . . . That's too much to ask. Policing was never meant to solve all those problems."

The Black Lives Matter movement and groups like the American Civil Liberties Union have called for comprehensive reforms that would shift some of those responsibilities to other agencies and organizations that they believe are better equipped to handle them. They ask questions such as: Should public money be used to hire police to handle discipline in schools, or should it go to hiring and training teachers and counselors? What are the pros and cons of each? Would the money be better spent investing in social services in poorer communities? This radical reimagining of large institutions echoes the calls made as far back as the 1960s by the Black Panthers, who put forth similar proposals to protect Black communities from police violence.

In 1970, Kent Ford, the founder of the Panthers chapter in Portland, Oregon, put forward a ballot proposal to his city council to have community members be part of a commission that would address policing in predominantly Black neighborhoods—a proposal very similar to some put forth by Black Lives Matter today. Fifty years later, he is

Jason Love, a police officer in St. Charles, Missouri–a suburb of St. Louis–speaks to protesters at a Black Lives Matter march on June 3, 2020.

on the front lines, still marching and protesting to keep his community safe. He told *The Oregonian,* "There's a chance [now to reform policing]. End homelessness. Get retraining. Education. Health care . . . That's why we have to stay in the streets. That's what's going to make it happen." He remains committed to the path he has followed for half a century—to push for change in his community.

On February 18, 2016, President Barack Obama held what he called an "intergenerational meeting" at the White House to discuss the findings of the policing task force. He wanted to gather Black Lives Matter activists and civil rights–era leaders to consider the future of law enforcement and other matters of race and class in the nation.

Obama himself had been in the position of both an inside man and an outside man. In the mid-'80s, before attending Harvard Law School, he spent three years as a community organizer in Chicago. He was twenty-four years old at the time and had grown up in Hawaii and Indonesia. Chicago was appealing to him in part because the city had recently elected its first Black mayor, Harold Washington. The future president got a job working for a group called the Developing Communities Project. For years, he went door-to-door, getting to know the people in the neighborhood and bringing community members and city officials together to address problems of environmental racism, such as asbestos exposure and water contamination. He would later refer to his years as an organizer as "the best education I ever had, better than anything I got at Harvard Law School."

Decades later he found himself on the other side of the equation. As the nation's first Black president, he had broken through to the highest office in the land, becoming the ultimate inside man. And at fifty-four, he was now the elder statesman while the Black Lives Matter leaders were the young community organizers agitating for change.

Not every young leader accepted his invitation. Aislinn Pulley, a leader with Black Lives Matter in the president's adopted hometown of Chicago, called the meeting "a sham" and said, "As a radical, Black organizer, living and working in a city that is now widely recognized as a symbol of corruption and police violence, I do not feel that a handshake with the president is the best way for me to honor Black History Month or the Black freedom fighters whose labor laid the groundwork for the historic moment we are living in."

But for Brittany Packnett Cunningham, opportunities to sit with the president of the United States and civil rights icons like Congressman John Lewis were too valuable to pass up. "I've always maintained that we have to take the fight everywhere," she said. "We have to leverage every single tool we have to get free."

First Lady Laura Bush, First Lady Michelle Obama, President Barack Obama, Representative John Lewis, President George W. Bush, and Representative Terri Sewell at a 2015 ceremony marking the fiftieth anniversary of Bloody Sunday, a violent attack on civil rights activists–including Lewis–who were marching for voting rights across the Edmund Pettus Bridge in Selma, Alabama.

At the meeting, the president gathered the leaders, both young and old, in the Roosevelt Room of the White House. In attendance were Lewis; Al Sharpton; Valerie Jarrett, senior adviser to the president; and Marc Morial, head of the National Urban League, as well as Mckesson and Packnett Cunningham. When Obama began the meeting, he extended a special welcome to the young activists who were "making history as we speak."

The group met for more than an hour and a half, discussing criminal justice reform and how to build a deeper degree of trust between law enforcement and the communities in which they serve.

Obama praised "the degree of focus and seriousness and constructiveness" that the younger activists brought. "They are much better organizers than I was when I was their age, and I am confident that they are going to take America to new heights," he said.

It was an important moment for the Black Lives Matter movement—one that showed its growing strength and legitimacy. It was also an opportunity for the younger activists to get an up-close lesson in leadership. Mckesson praised Obama for the way he brought the groups together, saying, "The president was really candid today. Not only did everyone get time to talk and engage, but there was also time to ask questions and go back and forth, not only with the president but also with senior staff."

After the meeting, Packnett Cunningham spoke to reporters about where the movement could go from there, using both the inside and outside approaches. "We can utilize so many tactics," she said. "Protest is incredibly important. Policy is incredibly important. It was important that there were real protesters in the room today and that this White House has continued to engage with protesters and activists across the country."

Like generations of activists who had come before them, the emerging leaders of Black Lives Matter found that there were many ways to do the work, and that there was no one way to lead a movement. By elevating the voices of community organizers around the country, Opal Tometi explained, Black Lives Matter took a "leaderful" approach, which empowered many members of the organization instead of putting the focus on a few well-known faces. It's a similar approach to the one taken by the civil rights leader Ella Baker, the architect of the Student Nonviolent Coordinating Committee (SNCC), which was an engine of nonviolent protest by young people in the 1960s. Baker believed that "strong people don't need strong leaders" and that movements benefited from having a wide range of organizers contributing to group decisions. Tometi agreed with that philosophy. In September 2020, she told *The Guardian:* "What we're trying to do now is be stronger than we ever were before. Leaders are everywhere. Yes, one might go, but there will be 10 more that pop up."

And her cofounders shared this sentiment. "We, Alicia, Opal and I, do not want to control it," Cullors writes in *When They Call You a Terrorist*. "We want it to spread like wildfire."

"WE HAVE TO LEVERAGE EVERY SINGLE TOOL WE HAVE TO GET FREE."

— Brittany Packnett Cunningham

A CHANGE IS GONNA COME

Martin Luther King knew a thing or two about what it takes to make lasting, systemic change. "The arc of the moral universe is long," he said, "but it bends toward justice." Activism in all its forms—from protests to lobbying to petitions to legal fights—is long, slow, difficult work. Looking at the history of the two most significant movements for racial justice in U.S. history—the Black liberation struggle of the 1950s and '60s, and Black Lives Matter—teaches us that change is possible when enough people stand up together and demand it. But these things take patience, resilience, unrelenting dedication—and, perhaps most of all, they take time. Here is a snapshot of some of the key moments during these two movements and the historical events that affected them.

The *New York Times* front page from May 18, 1954, announcing the Supreme Court's decision in *Brown v. Board of Education.*

CIVIL RIGHTS AND BLACK POWER, 1954–1968

Thurgood Marshall, then a lawyer for the National Association for the Advancement of Colored People (NAACP), standing with aides on December 11, 1952, outside the U.S. Supreme Court, where he was preparing to present his arguments in *Brown v. Board of Education*. In 1967, Marshall became the first Black justice to sit on the nation's highest court.

1954

- In *Brown v. Board of Education,* the Supreme Court rules that racial segregation in American public schools is unconstitutional, effectively overturning the doctrine of "separate but equal."

1955

- Emmett Till, a fourteen-year-old Black boy from Chicago, is murdered while visiting relatives in Mississippi. His lynching, and the published pictures of his body, spark national outrage.

- The activist Rosa Parks is arrested in Montgomery, Alabama, after refusing to give up her bus seat to a white passenger. Four days later, organizers led by Martin Luther King launch a boycott of the city's buses. It lasts more than a year, until the Supreme Court rules the segregated seating unconstitutional.

1957

- Escorted by U.S. Army and National Guard troops, a group of Black students known as the Little Rock Nine integrate Central High School in Arkansas.

1958

- Ella Baker, the first female president of the New York chapter of the National Association for the Advancement of Colored People (NAACP), moves to Atlanta to help organize the Southern Christian Leadership Conference (SCLC), which will mobilize many of the most significant mass protests of the civil rights era.

1959

- John Lewis, inspired by Martin Luther King, attends a series of workshops on nonviolent confrontation in Tennessee, where he meets Diane Nash. Together they help lead the

Rosa Parks outside the Montgomery, Alabama, courthouse on March 20, 1956, with E. D. Nixon, a local civil rights leader who helped organize the bus boycott.

Nashville Student Movement to desegregate the city's restaurants and other public facilities.

1960

- The Greensboro Four stage a sit-in at a Woolworth's lunch counter in North Carolina to protest segregation in restaurants. Similar sit-ins spread across the South, and, after five months of protests, the Woolworth's serves its first Black customer.

- Ella Baker organizes a meeting for the student leaders of the sit-ins, leading to the formation of the Student Nonviolent Coordinating Committee (SNCC), which is dedicated to civil disobedience by young people.

- President John F. Kennedy is elected.

- Six-year-old Ruby Bridges integrates William Frantz Elementary School in New Orleans, Louisiana.

1961

- The racially mixed "Freedom Riders"—including John Lewis and Stokely Carmichael—travel on buses into the Deep South to test enforcement of integration laws. When the Riders are arrested, Diane Nash recruits more organizers to keep the protest going.

1963

- James Baldwin publishes *The Fire Next Time,* his groundbreaking work on systemic racism.

- Martin Luther King is arrested at a protest in Alabama. In his cell, he writes "Letter from a Birmingham Jail"—one of the most important documents of the civil rights movement.

- Thousands of protesters participate in the March on Washington for Jobs and Freedom, where King gives his "I Have a Dream" speech.

Twelve-year-old Edith Lee-Payne at the March on Washington in 1963. Lee-Payne, who traveled from Detroit with her mother to participate in the protest, became a poster child for the civil rights movement. But she herself was not aware that this photo had been taken until her cousin spotted it in a Black history calendar in 2008.

- The Ku Klux Klan bombs the 16th Street Baptist Church in Birmingham, Alabama, killing four young girls who are attending Sunday school. Horrified by the terrorist attack, Diane Nash and her husband, James Bevel, begin planning the Alabama Project to register Black voters across the state.

- More than two hundred thousand young people in Chicago stage a one-day boycott, which they call Freedom Day, to demand equitable resources for Black students.

- President Kennedy is assassinated, and Lyndon B. Johnson takes office.

1964

- More than 450,000 Black and Puerto Rican students stage a boycott to protest inequality in New York's public schools.

- Nelson Mandela is sentenced to life in prison for protesting apartheid in South Africa.

- Over the course of the Freedom Summer, Black and white activists travel to Mississippi to register Black voters. Three of them—Andrew Goodman, James Chaney, and Michael Schwerner—are lynched.

- President Johnson signs the Civil Rights Act of 1964, which bans racial discrimination in employment and ends segregation in schools and public places, including restaurants and swimming pools.

- Riots break out in Harlem after James Powell, a fifteen-year-old Black boy, is fatally shot by the police. One person is killed, and hundreds of people are injured or arrested.

1965

- The activist Malcolm X is assassinated in New York. Unlike Martin Luther King, he was an early proponent of more militant protest, which would be adopted by the Black Power movement.

- In a violent confrontation now known as Bloody Sunday, protesters including John Lewis are beaten by a mob of angry citizens and Alabama state troopers while attempting to stage a voting rights march from Selma to Montgomery.

- President Johnson signs the Voting Rights Act of 1965, which bans discrimination at the polls on the basis of race.

1966

- Martin Luther King and the SCLC launch the Chicago Freedom Movement—the first significant expansion of their antiracist protest movement beyond the South.

- Stokely Carmichael, now the leader of SNCC, first uses the phrase "Black power" at a rally in Mississippi, signaling a split from King and other proponents of peaceful protest.

- The Black Panther Party for Self-Defense is founded in Oakland, California. Local chapters are started in cities across the country over the next decade.

1967

- Muhammad Ali defies the Vietnam draft.

WHERE LAW ENDS THERE TYRANNY BEG

Members of the Black Panther party were among some eight hundred people who gathered outside a Manhattan courthouse on April 11, 1969, to protest the indictment of four Panthers who were accused of planning to bomb several department stores and other sites around New York City.

- Newark, Detroit, and many other American cities experience a "long, hot summer" of racial unrest and riots.

- Martin Luther King announces the Poor People's Campaign, which he calls "the beginning of a new co-operation, understanding, and a determination by poor people of all colors and backgrounds to assert and win their right to a decent life and respect for their culture and dignity."

1968

- Martin Luther King is assassinated in Memphis, sparking uprisings across the country.

- President Johnson signs the Fair Housing Act, which outlaws discrimination by real estate agencies, banks, and other entities on the basis of race, religion, or national origin. It is later expanded to include gender, familial status, and disability.

- Arthur Ashe becomes the first Black tennis player to win the U.S. Open.

- The track athletes Tommie Smith and John Carlos raise their fists in a Black Power salute while accepting their medals at the Olympics in Mexico City.

Hundreds of protesters gather in Union Square in New York on March 21, 2012, as part of a Million Hoodie March to protest the killing of Trayvon Martin.

2012

- Trayvon Martin is shot and killed by George Zimmerman, a neighborhood watch volunteer, while walking home from a convenience store.

- The Dream Defenders, a coalition of Black and brown youth activists in Florida, stage a forty-mile protest march in response to Martin's death.

- Organizers in Florida launch the Million Hoodies Movement for Justice, calling for Zimmerman's arrest and for an end to gun violence, racial profiling, and police brutality.

- Barack Obama, the first Black president of the United States, is elected for a second term.

2013

- In *Shelby County v. Holder,* the Supreme Court strikes down many core tenets of the Voting Rights Act.

- George Zimmerman is acquitted in Trayvon Martin's death.

- After hearing the verdict, Alicia Garza writes a love letter to Black people on Facebook. She, Patrisse Cullors, and Opal Tometi launch a movement for racial justice under the hashtag #BlackLivesMatter.

- The Dream Defenders occupy the Florida state capitol for thirty-one days, calling for the repeal of the stand-your-ground laws that protected Zimmerman.

2014

- Eric Garner dies on Staten Island, New York, after being placed in a chokehold by Daniel Pantaleo, a white police officer.

- Michael Brown is shot and killed in Ferguson, Missouri, by Darren Wilson, a white police officer. His body is left in the street for hours.

- Protests erupt in Ferguson. Although they start as peaceful vigils, they soon escalate, with incidents of vandalism and looting and a violent police response. The uprisings continue for months and spread to more than 150 cities across the country.

- Inspired by the Freedom Rides of the 1960s, hundreds of activists, led by Darnell L. Moore and Patrisse Cullors, organize Black Lives Matter rides to Ferguson from all around the country.

- The activists Johnetta Elzie, DeRay Mckesson, Brittany Packnett Cunningham, and Justin Hansford start the *Ferguson Protester Newsletter*, which later becomes known as *This Is the Movement*.

- #BlackLivesMatter explodes on Twitter. In November, when a Ferguson grand jury decides not to indict Wilson in Brown's death, the hashtag is used 1.7 million times over the course of a few weeks.

- Tamir Rice, a twelve-year-old Black boy, is killed by a white police officer in Cleveland, Ohio.

- LeBron James, Kobe Bryant, and other NBA players, in memory of Garner, begin wearing I CAN'T BREATHE shirts during their pregame warm-ups.

Cleveland Cavaliers star LeBron James wears an I CAN'T BREATHE shirt in honor of Eric Garner during a warm-up for a game against the Brooklyn Nets on December 8, 2014.

- More than 150 Black congressional staffers stage a "Hands Up, Don't Shoot" walkout to protest Garner's and Brown's deaths.

- President Obama signs an executive order creating a Task Force on 21st Century Policing. Its members include Packnett Cunningham, a Missouri native and a leader in the Ferguson protests.

2015

- Black Lives Matter expands to include around forty local chapters across the country.

- The U.S. Department of Justice accuses Ferguson of a "pattern of unconstitutional policing" and calls on the city to overhaul its criminal justice system.

- Kendrick Lamar releases *To Pimp a Butterfly*. The album's seventh track, "Alright," becomes a Black Lives Matter anthem.

- Freddie Gray, a twenty-five-year-old Black man, dies in police custody in Baltimore, setting off another wave of Black Lives Matter protests.

- A coalition of organizers and activist groups in Cleveland holds the first convening of the Movement for Black Lives.

- Janelle Monáe releases the single "Hell You Talmbout," which calls attention to incidents of police brutality.

- DeRay Mckesson, Johnetta Elzie, Brittany Packnett Cunningham, and Samuel Sinyangwe found Campaign Zero, which pushes for research-based policy changes to end police brutality in the United States.

2016

- President Obama holds an "intergenerational meeting" of civil rights leaders and Black Lives Matter activists, including Brittany Packnett Cunningham and DeRay Mckesson, to discuss the findings of the policing task force.

- Twitter releases a list of the most-used hashtags related to social causes in its history. #Ferguson is number 1. #BlackLivesMatter is number 3. (Number 2 is #LoveWins, which celebrated the legalization of same-sex marriage in the United States in 2015.)

Protesters march outside a courthouse in Baltimore, Maryland, on September 2, 2015, as hearings begin in the trials of the six police officers charged in the death of Freddie Gray. None of them are convicted.

- Mckesson runs for mayor in Baltimore.

- The Movement for Black Lives publishes "A Vision for Black Lives," which outlines their proposals for ending systemic racism.

- Colin Kaepernick, a quarterback for the San Francisco 49ers, begins sitting during pregame performances of "The Star-Spangled Banner." He later switches to kneeling during the anthem to protest police brutality and racial injustice.

- Donald Trump is elected president.

2017

- On the day after President Trump's inauguration, millions of people participate in global Women's March demonstrations.

- Black Lives Matter activists participate in counterprotests against "Unite the Right," a white supremacist rally in Charlottesville, Virginia.

- Revelations of sexual misconduct by the Hollywood producer Harvey Weinstein kick off the #MeToo movement, which evolves into a nationwide reckoning against sexism, harassment, and abuse.

2018

- More than a million people, including many Black Lives Matter activists, join the student-led March for Our Lives protests against gun violence.

2019

- The basketball superstar Maya Moore steps away from the WNBA to devote her time to prison ministry and criminal justice reform.

- On an episode of his podcast *Why Is This Happening?* the journalist Chris Hayes asks Alicia Garza if Black Lives Matter's moment has passed. "I can tell you Black Lives Matter is still very much alive," she says. "I think what's hard is that people measure movements by how much they perform for you. So if there's not hundreds or thousands of people in the streets, there's no movement . . . There is all kinds of organizing that is still happening."

2020

- Ahmaud Arbery is fatally shot by two white men while he is jogging in his neighborhood in Glynn County, Georgia.

- The coronavirus pandemic takes hold, forcing the world into lockdown and killing hundreds of thousands of Americans.

- Breonna Taylor is killed in her home in Louisville, Kentucky, during a botched police raid.

- George Floyd is killed by a white Minneapolis police officer who kneels on his neck while Floyd pleads with him, saying, "I can't breathe." Protests erupt in the city and quickly spread.

- Three days after Floyd's death, the National Guard is deployed to Minneapolis to subdue the protests, which are turning increasingly volatile. At the same time, in Kentucky, the 911 call from Taylor's boyfriend is released, bringing her death into the national spotlight and setting off protests in Louisville.

- Derek Chauvin, the police officer who knelt on Floyd's neck, is arrested and charged with murder for his death.

- David McAtee, a Louisville barbecue shop owner, is shot and killed by the National Guard during a Black Lives Matter protest. Mayor Greg Fischer fires the city's police chief after learning that officers who were also involved in the shooting had their body cameras turned off.

- Black Lives Matter protests spread around the world, peaking on June 6.

- Around the world, statues honoring people tied to slavery or the Confederacy are removed or vandalized.

- The Minneapolis City Council vows to completely defund and dismantle its police department. But within a few months, council members begin to backtrack.

- The U.S. House of Representatives passes the George Floyd Justice in Policing Act of 2020, which includes a federal ban on chokeholds along with other criminal justice reforms. It stalls in the Senate when Republicans refuse to bring it up for a vote.

- The civil rights leader and renowned congressman John Lewis dies.

- The NBA, WNBA, and other professional sports leagues boycott games to protest the police shooting of Jacob Blake, a twenty-nine-year-old Black man who is paralyzed as a result, in Kenosha, Wisconsin.

- The tennis player Naomi Osaka wins her second U.S. Open. Throughout the tournament she wears face masks bearing the names of Black Americans who have been killed.

- Cori Bush, a nurse and Black Lives Matter activist from Ferguson, is elected to Congress, becoming the first Black representative in Missouri's history.

- Joe Biden defeats President Trump in the November election. His running mate, Kamala Harris, is the first Black person, Indian American, and woman to become vice president.

Kamala Harris celebrates her election as vice president in Wilmington, Delaware, on November 7, 2020. She is the first woman, first Black person, and first Indian American to hold the second-highest position in the U.S. government.

"At Segregated Drinking Fountain, Mobile, Alabama, 1956."

CHAPTER 5

WHAT IS SYSTEMIC RACISM?

What do you think about when you hear the word racist? Is it a person who uses a particular word or makes a joke that has a certain group of people as its punch line? Maybe you think about somebody who calls someone a name because of where they're from or the color of their skin. But those are just a few of the more obvious examples. What the Black Lives Matter activists sought to do was shift the national dialogue around race and justice, highlighting some of the less visible ways in which racism works.

As the movement grew, it quickly became clear that it was about more than just one incident or issue. According to *The Washington Post*—which, in the wake of Michael Brown's killing, began tracking all fatal shootings carried out by law enforcement—between January 2015 and June 2020, the police shot and killed more than fifty-four hundred people. During that period, Black Americans were killed by police at more than twice the rate of white Americans; Hispanic Americans were also disproportionately killed. The use of deadly force in cases like Brown's, activists argued, could not be written off as the unfortunate actions of racist individuals. They were the results of a system set up to oppress Black Americans. And ending this pattern of violence would require a more comprehensive approach that involved looking at these tragedies within the context of a deeply embedded history of racial inequality and injustice.

The Black Lives Matter movement powerfully connected the dots between the brutal violence of slavery, the legacy of an economy built on the subjugation of Black people, the decades of unjust systems and practices that rose up in the aftermath of the Civil War, and the inequality that continues to pervade society today. Organizers worked to broaden the conversation, urging Americans to consider how issues of race are woven into almost every aspect of life today, from schools and workplaces to neighborhoods and communities to hospitals and health care.

"When we say Black Lives Matter, we're talking about more than police brutality," Patrisse Cullors wrote in an article for the American Civil Liberties Union in June 2020. "We're talking about incarceration, health care, housing, education, and economics—all the different components of a broader system that has created the reality we see today . . . Black lives should matter in all stages of life— and to honor that truth, we must radically transform the system from its roots."

The task at hand was daunting: dismantling a rotten system that had served as the foundation of American society for centuries. But rather than despairing at the sheer scale of their goals, Black Lives Matter inspired millions of people, in the United States and around the world, by proclaiming the radical notion that ending systemic racism was not only necessary but possible.

To dismantle that system, the nation would have to

A young boy is confronted by National Guard troops in Newark, New Jersey, on July 14, 1967. Newark was one of several American cities where protests against police brutality and racial injustice broke out in the "long, hot summer" of 1967. The unrest in Newark, which started after a Black cab-driver was brutally beaten by police, was among the deadliest in the nation: in just six days, twenty-six people–most of them Black– were killed and more than seven hundred were injured.

go back to the beginning and grapple with how it was built in the first place. In the United States, slavery is usually taught and discussed as an atrocity that happened a long time ago, mainly in the South, the journalist Nikole Hannah-Jones writes in *The 1619 Project,* an ambitious work of journalism published by *The New York Times Magazine* in 2019 that seeks to excavate and interrogate this history. Slavery in the United States is older than the country itself. It precedes the Declaration of Independence by more than 150 years and was foundational to almost every aspect of American life—in every region, not just the South. "The United States is a nation founded on both an ideal and a lie," Hannah-Jones explains. The Declaration of Independence may have proclaimed that "all men are created equal," but, she writes, "the white men who drafted those words did not believe them to be true for the hundreds of thousands of black people in their midst. 'Life, Liberty and the pursuit of Happiness' did not apply to fully one-fifth of the country."

But the legacy of slavery is still apparent today. In *The 1619 Project,* Hannah-Jones and her colleagues argue—as many academics, economists, historians, and public policy experts have for decades—that slavery has been the financial, moral, social, and emotional underpinning of life in the United States from the beginning. As the opinion columnist Jamelle Bouie writes in *The 1619 Project,* "America holds onto an undemocratic assumption from its founding—that some people deserve more power than others."

From 1619 to 1865, wealth among white Americans was largely built on the unpaid labor of enslaved people, which brought tens of millions of dollars into the economy. "Nearly one-fourth of all white Southerners owned slaves, and upon their backs the economic basis of America—and much of the Atlantic world—was erected," Ta-Nehisi Coates explains in "The Case for Reparations," his seminal 2014 essay for *The Atlantic.* Cotton, which was produced primarily by the labor of enslaved people on plantations, made up around 59 percent of all U.S. exports by the mid-1800s. Across the seven main cotton-producing states in the South, one-third of all white income came from slavery.

And even states whose economies didn't revolve around plantation agriculture benefited from this system. "In the decades between the American Revolution and the Civil War, slavery—as a source of the cotton that fed Rhode Island's mills, as a source of the wealth that filled New York's banks, as a source of the markets that inspired Massachusetts' manufacturers—proved indispensable to national economic development," the historians Sven Beckert and Seth Rockman write in *Slavery's Capitalism: A New History of American Economic Development.*

"AMERICA HOLDS ONTO AN UNDEMOCRATIC ASSUMPTION FROM ITS FOUNDING — THAT SOME PEOPLE DESERVE MORE POWER THAN OTHERS."

— Jamelle Bouie

The Union won the Civil War in 1865—in part thanks to the service of Black soldiers and freedom fighters—and slavery in the United States was abolished. Four million Black Americans officially gained their freedom. But white landowners quickly constructed a system ensuring that they could continue to employ Black people and pay them almost nothing for their work. These laws were called the Black Codes, and between 1865 and 1866 almost all Southern states enacted them. In order to obtain any kind of work, Black people were forced to sign contracts with white employers that paid them pennies. If they didn't have contracts, they were considered "vagrants" and could be fined or thrown in prison. And if they broke their contracts and sought positions with better pay elsewhere, the contract holders could force them to work without any pay at all. The Black Codes were enforced by all-white law enforcement patrols—predecessors to today's police departments—that were largely made up of former Confederate soldiers and former members of slave patrols.

During this era, violence against Black Americans surged, and they had few protections. The Black Codes meant that policing, such as it was, was set up not to protect Black people, but to maintain a hierarchy that mirrored as closely as possible the power imbalances of the slavery era. It was during this time that the Ku Klux Klan was founded in Pulaski, Tennessee, as a club for Confederate men. It quickly became a secret society that terrorized Black Americans. The members included people from all social and economic classes.

After the Black Codes, white lawmakers crafted legislation known as Jim Crow laws, which ensured that Black Americans were firmly and almost permanently entrenched in the lower classes because of the color of their skin. Nominally, Jim Crow laws were about separating Black and white people. This was the beginning of nearly one hundred years of segregation, the separate and unequal policies that affected everything from where a person could work to where they could live, what kind of health care they received, what types of schools they attended, and, later, even such things as where they could go dancing or see a movie.

Jim Crow was more than just a set of laws. It created a society of violence and fear that oppressed Black people. Lynching—the practice of killing someone, often publicly, knowing that this crime will go unpunished because of the victim's race—was a key part of this. Mobs of white people regularly killed Black Americans, and the police didn't simply look the other way: sometimes they encouraged or even actively participated in the violence. In many cases, groups like the Klan targeted Black people who were high achievers—*because* of their education or growing wealth—as a way of protecting the political and economic power of white people and maintaining the status quo of Black Americans as second-class citizens.

These kinds of oppression weren't limited to the South. And though there were fewer explicitly segregationist laws in other parts of the country, systems such as redlining had many of the same practical effects. This real estate practice, in which certain predominantly Black neighborhoods were designated by the government as "high risk," prevented many Black Americans from getting mortgages from banks and thus from owning their homes. In many places they also weren't allowed to buy houses in more affluent, predominantly white neighborhoods, which in turn limited their access to better-funded public schools and other municipal services. White flight from the cities—white residents leaving areas where more and more Black people moved in—combined with redlining and other practices kept many of America's neighborhoods basically segregated long after such policies had been officially outlawed, including into the twenty-first century.

Redlining and other practices created segregated neighborhoods in many northern cities. A photographer for *Look* magazine captured the Jackson family as they went house-hunting in Philadelphia in 1956. This block was part of a "whites-only" neighborhood.

From left, Rosa Parks, the Reverend Ralph Abernathy, Juanita Abernathy, Ralph Bunche, Martin Luther King, and Coretta Scott King during a voting rights march from Selma to Montgomery, Alabama, in March 1965. This image ran on the cover of *Ebony* magazine that May.

Black Americans were also systematically denied the right to vote. After the end of slavery, the Fourteenth and Fifteenth Amendments established voting rights for free Black men, many of whom were eager to go to the polls. (At the time, women of any race were still unable to vote.) But states across the country, and particularly in the South, quickly put in place new laws, prohibitively expensive poll taxes, literacy tests, and other means of intimidation meant to keep Black Americans from voting, holding political office, or serving on juries—essentially shutting them out of the political system. According to the historian Gilda Daniels, in 1890, there were 140,000 Black men in Alabama who were registered to vote. By 1906, that number had fallen to forty-six.

Deprived of a voice in the political system, Black Americans would have to use tools like marches, sit-ins, speeches, and boycotts to make their voices heard. In the 1950s and 1960s, activists including Martin Luther King, Ella Baker, John Lewis, Diane Nash, Rosa Parks, Malcolm X, and Stokely Carmichael rallied thousands of people to fight for civil rights. They used the power of protest to pressure lawmakers to change the racist policies that had kept Black people from America's promises of life, liberty, and the pursuit of happiness for so long. Landmark laws like the Civil Rights Act of 1964, the Voting Rights Act of 1965, and the Fair Housing Act of 1968—along with rulings by the Supreme Court in cases such as *Brown v. Board of Education*—helped dismantle the racist framework of Jim Crow and establish legal protections for Black Americans in schools, in the workplace, in their homes, and at the ballot box. The changes these activists were able to enact were extraordinary, and, on paper, they broke down the caste system that for so long had oppressed nonwhite Americans. But changing public opinion about the treatment of Black people and the need for antiracist policies was more challenging. Well after the 1960s, there is still a lot of work to do to root out the racism built into the foundations of American society.

In economic terms, wealth continues to be distributed

The civil rights organizer Virginius Bray Thornton III leads a protest at Atlanta University in 1960. That April, the activist Ella Baker invited hundreds of young organizers such as Thornton who had orchestrated the sit-in movement to integrate dining establishments across the South to a meeting at Shaw University in Raleigh, North Carolina. There, they formed the Student Nonviolent Coordinating Committee (SNCC), which would go on to guide much of the youth-powered activism of the civil rights movement.

In September 1957, fifteen-year-old Elizabeth Eckford was among the group of nine Black students who integrated the formerly all-white Little Rock Central High School in Arkansas. A white mob hurled obscenities and racial slurs at Eckford and the rest of the Little Rock Nine as they attempted to enter the school. Eventually, President Dwight Eisenhower had to send in U.S. Army and National Guard troops to protect the students as they attended classes.

in ways that are deeply shaped by systemic racism. In the fifty-plus years since the Civil Rights Act, there has been little progress in the economic security of Black Americans, who continue to be denied the opportunities and economic mobility available to white people. A 2019 study by the U.S. Federal Reserve found that the average white family has nearly eight times the wealth of the average Black family. To put it another way, for every dollar the average white family holds, the average Black family has less than fifteen cents.

The persistence of systemic racism can also be seen in schools. Researchers have found that bias, including the disproportionate targeting for punishment of Black Americans, begins as early as preschool. One study by the U.S. Department of Education found that Black kids make up only 18 percent of all preschoolers but constitute 42 percent of kids who are suspended in preschool. As students get older, the divide continues. Even when kids are being punished for breaking similar rules, Black kids are suspended nearly four times as often as white kids.

These lingering effects of the legacy of slavery and Jim Crow are what Black Lives Matter seeks to remedy. At its core, the movement is about an idea overwhelmingly large—the promise of racial justice—and something so simple: how Black Americans of all ages, genders, and walks of life can live well and freely on a daily basis. As Alicia Garza put it, the creation of Black Lives Matter "absolutely was about: how do we live in a world that dehumanizes us and still be human? The fight is not just being able to keep breathing. The fight is actually to be able to walk down the street with your head held high—and feel like I belong here, or I deserve to be here, or I just have [the] right to have a level of dignity."

Students in New York staging a boycott on February 3, 1964, to protest inequality in the city's schools, which remained largely divided along racial lines even a decade after *Brown v. Board of Education* made school segregation illegal. Racial inequality continues to be an issue in New York schools today.

"I am not going to stand up to show pride in a flag for a country that oppresses Black people and people of color," Colin Kaepernick, seen kneeling with his teammate Eric Reid during the national anthem before a game in 2016, told a reporter for *NFL Media*. "To me, this is bigger than football, and it would be selfish on my part to look the other way."

CHAPTER 6

HOW CHAMPIONS LEAD

As long as there have been professional sports in America, they have been shaped by both racism and struggles for racial justice, many of which have played out on the tennis court, the Olympic podium, or the football field.

In 2016, Colin Kaepernick, a quarterback for the San Francisco 49ers, was upset by the seemingly constant reports of Black Americans being killed by police. Wanting to understand the history of racial injustice in this country, he did his homework, reading such books as *The Fire Next Time* by James Baldwin, *The Autobiography of Malcolm X,* and *I Know Why the Caged Bird Sings* by Maya Angelou.

These books spoke with poetry and precision of the many years for which Black Americans had been struggling for equality and of all the hurdles they had faced. Kaepernick found clarity and purpose in their words—from Baldwin's letters to his teenage nephew urging him to confront systemic racism, to Angelou's call to pursue justice, to Malcolm X's conviction that all humanity must join together and fight together for freedom. "I've had enough of someone else's propaganda," the civil rights leader writes in his autobiography. "I'm for truth, no matter who tells it. I'm for justice, no matter who it is for or against. I'm a human being first and foremost, and as such I'm for whoever and whatever benefits humanity as a whole."

These books had a profound effect on Kaepernick, who felt he was receiving an education that contradicted so much of what he had been taught as a kid. In a press conference, the twenty-eight-year-old quarterback told reporters,

"This country stands for freedom, liberty, justice for all, and it's not happening for all right now."

Unable to pledge allegiance to a country that he felt had broken its core promise—to treat all its citizens as if they were created equal—he started sitting on the sidelines while the rest of the stadium sang "The Star-Spangled Banner" before the 49ers' games. His protest quickly caught the attention of the media. Some outraged fans felt that Kaepernick's actions were disrespectful, even accusing him of being un-American. Kaepernick and his teammate Eric Reid consulted with Nate Boyer, a former NFL player and decorated U.S. Army veteran, who suggested that they kneel rather than sit during the playing of the anthem. "We chose to kneel because it's a respectful gesture," wrote Reid, who joined Kaepernick in taking a knee, in *The New York Times* in 2017. "I remember thinking our posture was like a flag flown at half-mast to mark a tragedy." Kaepernick also pledged to donate $1 million to organizations fighting for social justice in marginalized communities.

The switch to kneeling wasn't enough to appease some of Kaepernick's most vocal critics. Fans posted videos of themselves burning his jersey. Bob McNair, the owner of the Houston Texans, denounced the protest, saying, "We can't have the inmates running the prison"—a comment many thought showed how he felt about Black players. And President Donald Trump fanned the flames, declaring that Kaepernick should be expelled from the NFL.

Still, many scholars pointed out that the national anthem itself, like so much of American history, was tainted by a complex history of racism. As the historian and writer Jelani Cobb explained in *The New Yorker:* "It's kind of an irony that we find ourselves criticizing now predominantly Black athletes for issuing a statement of dissent in the context of the national anthem. Given Francis Scott Key's own racial sympathies—or lack thereof."

Key, who wrote "The Star-Spangled Banner," was a slaveholder who referred to Black Americans as "a distinct and inferior race of people, which all experience proves to be the greatest evil that afflicts a community." And while only the first stanza of his anthem, with its rockets and bombs bursting, is typically played at events, the song actually goes on for several verses, and some historians—including Harry Edwards, Kaepernick's mentor and a professor emeritus at the University of California, Berkeley—point to them as further evidence of Key's racism. In the third verse, Key writes:

No refuge could save the hireling and slave
From the terror of flight or the gloom of the grave:
And the star-spangled banner in triumph doth wave
O'er the land of the free and the home of the brave.

"I'M FOR TRUTH, NO MATTER WHO TELLS IT. I'M FOR JUSTICE, NO MATTER WHO IT IS FOR OR AGAINST. I'M A HUMAN BEING FIRST AND FOREMOST."

— Malcolm X

While some scholars disagree, Edwards and others interpret these lyrics as a call for the execution of people who dare to run away from their enslavers. Black Americans, Edwards explained, struggle to embrace an anthem that does not count them among the free or brave. "African Americans are very much willing to accept what the first stanza of the song has become," he said. "But they also insist that we live up to it."

The 49ers dropped Kaepernick, ultimately paying him less than a third of the $126 million they had promised him in 2014. As of this writing, he has not played in the NFL for four years—longer than the average player's entire career. His athletic dreams were effectively cut short by his principles. But support for his protest, and for the issues that compelled him to kneel, has only continued to grow—even within the league itself.

In the summer of 2020, the NFL's commissioner, Roger Goodell, under pressure as more and more players expressed support for the Black Lives Matter protests rocking the nation, expressed some remorse for the way the league had rejected Kaepernick. "I wish we had listened earlier, Kaep, to what you were kneeling about and what you were trying to bring attention to," he said.

While some athlete activists have been forced to cut their careers short, others have done so voluntarily in order to work on behalf of causes they care about. Maya Moore is one of the most talented athletes ever to play the game of basketball. A college champion, she went on to win four WNBA titles and two Olympic gold medals. But in February 2019, she announced that she was stepping away from the sport she loved in order to devote a year to "some ministry dreams that have been stirring in my heart for many years." In January 2020, she extended that leave to focus on the appeals case of Jonathan Irons, a Black man she and her family had met in 2007 while volunteering with a prison ministry program, and whom they believed had been wrongly imprisoned.

When Irons was sixteen, he was arrested and convicted

In 2017, the WNBA star Maya Moore–along with Mark Dupree, a district attorney from Kansas, and Miriam Krinsky, a former federal prosecutor–cowrote an op-ed in *USA Today* calling for a reimagining of the American criminal justice system. "We feel a responsibility to make the most of our platforms and our privilege by demanding that those around us–those who come to our games to support us, those who voted for us, or those in our neighborhood who have high hopes that we will bring a higher level of thinking to our criminal justice system–are treated with respect, dignity, and fairness," they wrote.

of burglary and assault with a deadly weapon. He maintained that he was innocent, that he hadn't even been at the scene when the crime happened, and that the confession used to convict him had been coerced by the police. There were no corroborating witnesses, fingerprints, or DNA tying him to the crime, but a jury found him guilty anyway. He had already served twenty-three years of a fifty-year sentence when Moore, at the peak of her career, announced that she was taking time off from professional basketball

to work on his case. Moore and her family believed that, in securing Irons's freedom, they could show the many ways in which the criminal justice system failed Black people like him.

Even though Irons was only sixteen, he was tried as an adult, and a prosecutor in his case used language that many believed biased the jury against Irons because of his race. "Don't be soft on him because he is young," the lawyer instructed the jury. "He is as dangerous as somebody five times that age. We need to send a message to some of these younger people that if you are going to act like somebody old, you are going to be treated like somebody old."

That phrase "some of these younger people" is key. Black youths are more than four times more likely to be convicted of crimes than their white counterparts. A study by the Sentencing Project found that arrests of white people under the age of eighteen fell by 49 percent between 2003 and 2013, in part thanks to public policy changes that focused on early intervention and prioritized rehabilitative measures—such as counseling and community service—over incarceration for nonviolent crimes. But during that same time period, arrests of Black youths fell by just 31 percent, and they continued to be arrested at around twice the rate of young white people.

In 2016, the summer before Colin Kaepernick began

kneeling during the national anthem, Moore and her team-mates began wearing black T-shirts over their jerseys during warm-ups before their games. The fronts of the shirts read CHANGE STARTS WITH US: JUSTICE AND ACCOUNTABILITY. The backs said BLACK LIVES MATTER.

As she embarked on her sabbatical year, Moore told *The New York Times* that she was stepping away to focus on a cause larger than championship rings. She wanted to use her fame to spread the message that "Black and brown bodies are more vulnerable because of our country's history, that our justice system has historically operated from a racist spirit. It is true, but not an acknowledged truth."

On July 1, 2020, Irons walked out of prison a free man. A judge had overturned his conviction, pointing to a series of issues in his original trial. Moore was waiting for him with open arms. "I feel like I can live life now," Irons said. Two months later, he and Moore revealed that, over the last few years of working on his appeal, what had started as a partnership and friendship had grown into something more and that, shortly after Irons's release, they had gotten married. "Over time, it was pretty clear what the Lord was doing in our hearts," Moore told the journalist Robin Roberts on *Good Morning America,* "and now we're sitting here today, starting a whole new chapter." The couple promised to continue fighting for justice, together.

Kaepernick and Moore are both part of a long lineage of athletes who have used their platforms to fight for causes they care about. In 1967, Muhammad Ali was on top of the world: an Olympic gold medalist, heavyweight champion, and cultural icon. But on April 28 of that year, the legendary boxer announced that he was refusing to be drafted into the U.S. Army to fight in the Vietnam War. Ali, who had joined the Nation of Islam, objected on religious grounds to participating in a conflict he did not support. He told reporters: "The real enemy of my people is here. I will not disgrace my religion, my people, or myself by becoming a tool to enslave those who are fighting for their own justice, freedom, and equality."

Ali was stripped of his championship titles, banned from boxing, indicted for draft-dodging, and sentenced to prison. It took more than three years for his conviction to be overturned, unanimously, by the Supreme Court and for him to be allowed to return to competition. But his refusal to abandon his principles cost him precious time. He returned to boxing in 1970, but the dominance he had built was gone. He managed to reclaim his heavyweight title in 1974, but it was harder. The trademark speed and agility of the man who could "float like a butterfly, sting like a bee" didn't come as easily as they had in the years of his prime. They'd been sacrificed to a cause greater than himself.

Muhammad Ali in New York in 1969, two years after he refused the draft. Eulogizing the boxing great at his funeral in 2016, President Barack Obama said of Ali: "His fight outside the ring would cost him his title and his public standing. It would earn him enemies on the left and the right, make him reviled, and nearly send him to jail. But Ali stood his ground. And his victory helped us get used to the America we recognize today."

In 1968, at the Olympics in Mexico City, Tommie Smith and John Carlos, two Black track athletes, also found themselves in the spotlight when they came in first and third in the two-hundred-meter dash. But while they were held up as America's best at the games, they faced a far different reality back home. Martin Luther King had been assassinated just a few months earlier, and racial tensions in the United States were high, with riots and protests gripping cities across the country. Smith and Carlos may have been on the podium for the moment, but they knew that when

A protester holds up a sign at the 1968 Olympic trials for track and field in Los Angeles. During the run-up to that fall's games in Mexico City, the Olympic Project for Human Rights, led by Harry Edwards (who would later become Colin Kaepernick's mentor), encouraged Black athletes to boycott the Olympics to protest the treatment of Black people in countries such as the United States and South Africa.

they returned home, they would go back to being treated as second-class citizens because of their skin color.

Before the competition, the two men had joined the Olympic Project for Human Rights, which called for measures like hiring more Black coaches and banning countries such as South Africa that practiced a form of segregation known as apartheid. The runners debated whether to boycott the Olympics altogether in protest but decided instead that they would use the platform of the games to make a statement while the eyes of the world were on them. "We had to be seen because we couldn't be heard," Smith told *Smithsonian* magazine in 2008.

At the ceremony where they accepted their gold and bronze medals, Smith and Carlos raised their black-gloved fists in the air during the playing of "The Star-Spangled Banner." The third athlete on the podium—the white Australian silver medalist Peter Norman—stood with them in solidarity, wearing a badge from the Olympic Project for Human Rights. The men's raised fists were a salute to Black Power and resilience and a rejection of a system of deep inequality. (The raised fist would also become a popular symbol of solidarity within the Black Lives Matter movement.)

Like Ali—and Kaepernick—Smith and Carlos faced an immediate backlash. The stadium erupted in jeers, and they were suspended from the U.S. Olympic team and kicked out of the Olympic Village. When they went home, they faced a smear campaign and death threats. In time, however, their salute came to be seen as a bold act of peaceful protest. And Smith and Carlos remained undeterred in their fight for justice. "What I did was right 48 years ago, and 48 years

Despite the public backlash to their protest, Tommie Smith and John Carlos never wavered in their belief that they had done the right thing. "We experienced a lot of pain the rest of our lives. Now the wounds are healed, but you still see scars," Smith told *The New York Times* in 1996. "If I hadn't done what I did, I'd have a job, but no soul, no mind, and no heart," Carlos added. "Wouldn't I be worse off?"

later it has proven to be right," Carlos told *The Telegraph* in 2016. "In 1968, we were on a program for humanity—we are still on the same program today."

For Smith and Carlos, and many other athletes, the political was personal. The same year that they raised their fists, a twenty-five-year-old army lieutenant named Arthur Ashe became the first Black player to win the U.S. Open. Ashe, who would go on to become a tennis superstar, was determined to bring awareness to causes that had few champions. "From what we get, we can make a living," he once said. "What we give, however, makes a life."

Ashe challenged racial bias against Haitian refugees and fought against apartheid. He spoke at rallies, wrote pieces for newspapers, and advocated for sanctions against South Africa. In 1985, he and forty-six other activists were arrested for protesting outside the South African embassy in Washington, DC. Ashe was inspired, in part, by the examples of Ali, Smith, and Carlos. In his memoir he wrote that he admired how these men "had stood tall against the sky and had insisted on being heard on matters other than boxing or track and field, on weighty matters of civil rights and social responsibility and the destiny of black Americans in the modern world."

Then, in 1992, during a time when AIDS was still stigmatized as a disease that disproportionately affected

gay men, Ashe, who was straight, revealed to the public that he had contracted the disease through a blood transfusion. He immediately threw himself into raising money for AIDS research, using his popularity as a tennis player to inspire donations that the fight against the disease had rarely received.

Even as AIDS took its toll on Ashe's once powerfully athletic body, he continued to protest. In September 1992, at a rally in support of Haitian refugees, he marched through the nation's capital wearing a T-shirt that said HAITIANS LOCKED OUT BECAUSE THEY'RE BLACK. Ashe was arrested in front of the White House, handcuffed, and dragged off to jail. The next night, after he was released and made it home to New York, he started experiencing chest pains. It turned out that he'd had a heart attack—his second. But until his death, in 1993, he kept showing up and protesting.

And his legacy continues. In August 2020, the twenty-two-year-old tennis player Naomi Osaka, the daughter of a Haitian American father and a Japanese mother, walked into Arthur Ashe Stadium in Queens for her third U.S. Open, hoping to reclaim the title she had won in 2018

but lost the following summer. She came with seven face masks in her bag—each emblazoned with the name of a Black person who had died either in an interaction with the police or in a racially motivated crime. Earlier in the summer, Osaka had attended a Black Lives Matter rally in Minneapolis. She also refused to play her semifinal match in the Western and Southern Open, joining a multisport boycott by athletes who were protesting the police shooting of yet another Black man, Jacob Blake, in Kenosha, Wisconsin.

At her first match in September, Osaka broke out her first mask, which was emblazoned with the name of Breonna Taylor, the Black emergency room technician killed in a botched police raid in Louisville, Kentucky—Ali's hometown—in March 2020. Over the next several matches Osaka continued to use the platform of the tournament to draw attention to the names of other Black Americans who had been killed: Elijah McClain, Ahmaud Arbery, Trayvon Martin, George Floyd, Philando Castile, Tamir Rice. In her post-match press conferences, she spoke of the victims of gun violence and police brutality whose names she wore, and of her conviction to do whatever she could to amplify their stories. "I'm aware that tennis is watched all over the world," she said, "and maybe there is someone that doesn't know Breonna Taylor's story."

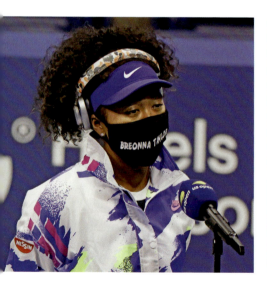

Osaka won match after match and shared name after name. When she won the final on September 12, reclaiming her title, her mask bore the seventh and final name: Tamir Rice, a twelve-year-old Black boy who was killed by a police officer in Cleveland in 2014. And across social media, as people celebrated her victory, they were also saying his name.

At each match during the 2020 U.S. Open, Naomi Osaka wore a face mask bearing the name of a Black American who had been killed by gun violence or in an interaction with police. "The point is to make people start talking," she said at the awards ceremony where she claimed her second women's singles title.

A Black Lives Matter march in Williamsburg, Brooklyn, on June 7, 2020, turned into a dance party, complete with a DJ and a singer who led the crowd in a call-and-response hymn.

CHAPTER 7

LIFT EVERY VOICE AND SING

If you go to a Black Lives Matter march, you will hear chants that ring out across the crowds. Someone begins a call, and the people respond, a rhythm slowly building that echoes the footsteps of the march.

Whose streets?

Our streets!

Whose streets?

Our streets!

I say, "Black Lives!"
You say, "Matter!"
Black Lives!

Matter!

Black Lives!

Matter!

Anyone can start the refrain, and then the community joins in harmony to lift their voices in a resounding chorus.

Show me what democracy looks like.

This is what democracy looks like!

Show me what America looks like.

This is what America looks like!

Show me what solidarity looks like.

This is what solidarity looks like!

Throughout the history of the Black struggle for freedom, music—especially the kind made by human voices—has been a powerful tool of protest. The chants heard at today's marches draw on the tradition of early American church music and spirituals, styles that have been refined by Black people since the days of enslavement. Sung in the fields while enslaved people were at work, this music carries the rhythm of manual labor in its bones, but its harmonies are those of defiance and resilience, of a longing for freedom and the hope and determination to make that dream a reality.

Frederick Douglass, the abolitionist and activist, spoke of the importance of songs during the days of Black enslavement. To an ignorant observer, he writes in his book *My Bondage and My Freedom,* spirituals appeared to be simple hymns, retelling biblical stories and themes. But the songs held deeper meaning for the people who sang them, acting as coded messages that passed along information about how one might escape and serving as much-needed reminders that freedom was *possible.* "A keen observer might have detected in our repeated singing of 'O Canaan, sweet Canaan, I am bound for the land of Canaan' something more than a hope of reaching heaven," Douglass writes. "We meant to reach the north." Many popular spirituals had these double meanings, with rallying cries and messages of justice and hope hidden within their symbolic lyrics. Take another example he cites from that era: "I thought I heard them say/There were lions in the way/I don't expect to stay/Much longer here." Douglass explains that, for enslaved people, this wasn't just a song about the biblical journey of the Israelites: it was an anthem promising "a speedy pilgrimage toward a free state, and a deliverance from all the evils and dangers of slavery."

The legacy of these spirituals continued after the abolition of slavery—particularly in blues music, which emerged in the South in the wake of the Civil War and rose to prominence in the late 1800s and early 1900s. Blues songs spoke to the lived experience of Black Americans during the era of Jim Crow. Their lyrics were typically in the first person, but the stories they told—of poverty and heartbreak, violence and discrimination, resilience and love—were universal. And through their music, blues performers such as Bessie Smith affirmed for Black Americans that their experiences deserved to be heard. "By singing about black lives with care and conviction," the journalist Maureen Mahon wrote for *NPR,* "Smith and her sister classic blues women Ma Rainey, Alberta Hunter and Sippie Wallace advanced the revolutionary idea that black lives mattered—and specifically, that black *women's* lives mattered."

In 1939, a young jazz singer from Philadelphia named Billie Holiday turned the spotlight of her talent on one of the darkest corners of American history: the horrors of lynching. The song she sang was called "Strange Fruit." And its lyrics were haunting, painting a visceral picture of Black bodies swinging from a blood-soaked tree somewhere in the South.

The song was written by Abel Meeropol, a white, Jewish high school teacher in the Bronx, who published its verses as a poem under the title "Bitter Fruit" in *New York Teacher* magazine, a union publication for city teachers. Meeropol was compelled to write the song after seeing a 1930 photo taken in Indiana in which white men and women stood,

some smiling for the camera, in front of Thomas Shipp and Abe Smith. The two Black men hung lifeless from a tree, nooses around their necks.

Meeropol set his words to music, and the song made its way to Barney Josephson, the owner of Café Society—a club whose tagline was "The Wrong Place for the Right People."

When Billie Holiday, pictured in 1947, sang "Strange Fruit" at the end of her sets at Café Society, the room was completely dark and silent–except for the spotlight on her face and the sound of her voice. "People had to remember 'Strange Fruit,' get their insides burned with it," said the club's owner, Barney Josephson.

Josephson knew that the song was shocking. Jazz was wildly popular at the time, and it had never so overtly taken on racial violence, but he felt it was important that the multiracial audiences at his club hear it in a way that made them directly confront its meaning. So he asked Holiday, who was then only twenty-three years old, to close each of her sets with it. In addition, he asked the waiters to stop serving before she began and for the room to be totally dark, except for a spotlight on Holiday.

Dorian Lynskey, author of *33 Revolutions Per Minute: A History of Protest Songs,* writes that when Holiday sang the song, the powerful lyrics "infected the air in the room, cut conversation stone dead, left drinks untouched, cigarettes unlit. Customers either clapped till their hands were sore, or walked out in disgust."

"Strange Fruit" proved that a protest song could be more than an anthem: it could be art. Sixty years later, it remained so iconic that *Time* magazine named it the Best Song of the Twentieth Century.

During the civil rights movement, music took center stage. At the March on Washington for Jobs and Freedom in 1963, the folk singer Joan Baez led the crowd of thousands in the singing of the gospel song "We Shall Overcome." Based on an old spiritual, an early version of which was published in 1901 by the Reverend Dr. Charles Albert Tindley, the song was turned into a political anthem by striking tobacco factory workers in the 1940s, and it became a rallying cry of the civil rights movement. It spoke to the protesters' struggle and their determination that, though it might be slow work, justice would eventually prevail:

We shall overcome;
We shall overcome;
We shall overcome some day.

Oh, deep in my heart
I do believe
We shall overcome some day.

Just as the first spirituals had given hope to enslaved Black Americans and united them in their struggle for freedom, the new hymns of the civil rights movement were an energizing force that rang with the protesters' determination to fight for equality. One of the most popular gospel songs of the era, "Lift Every Voice and Sing," became known as the Black national anthem. It spoke to this slow fight to bend the arc of history toward justice. Its lyrics—taken from a poem written in 1900 by James Weldon Johnson, who would later lead the National Association for the Advancement of Colored People (NAACP)—were both a battle cry and a vow that bound those who sang it together in the struggle:

Sing a song full of the faith that the dark past has taught us,

Sing a song full of the hope that the present has brought us;

Facing the rising sun of our new day begun,

Let us march on 'til victory is won.

Music was an important part of the 1963 March on Washington, from spontaneous songs by protesters like these to performances by the gospel legend Mahalia Jackson, the opera singer Marian Anderson, and folk musicians including Bob Dylan and Joan Baez.

The lineage of protest music has continued into the age of Black Lives Matter. It shines through, for example, in "Alright," the fourth single from the rapper Kendrick Lamar's 2015 album, *To Pimp a Butterfly*. In a 2016 interview for *GQ* magazine, Lamar told the music producer Rick Rubin that even before he wrote the lyrics, he heard something deeper within the catchy beats laid down by Pharrell Williams.

Lamar had recently visited South Africa, and the song began to take shape for him on Robben Island, where the activist Nelson Mandela was imprisoned for eighteen of the twenty-seven years he spent behind bars for challenging the brutal system of apartheid. The lyrics to "Alright" draw on this history of the struggle for racial justice, and they speak to the resilience of Black people who have continued to fight for freedom, undeterred, in the face of violence, suppression, and other systemic obstacles throughout history.

"Alright" became an anthem of the Black Lives Matter movement during a time when it needed hope and encouragement. In the years before the issues these activists raised took center stage, Lamar used his platform to spread their message.

As he told *NPR:* "Four hundred years ago, as slaves, we prayed and sung joyful songs to keep our heads level-headed with what was going on. Four hundred years later,

The rapper Kendrick Lamar performs in 2015. His song "Alright," released that June, became an anthem of the Black Lives Matter movement. According to *Billboard,* at the height of the protests in early June 2020, the song was streamed more than one million times in a single day.

"SILENCE IS OUR ENEMY, BUT SOUND IS OUR WEAPON."

— Janelle Monáe

A few months after Lamar released "Alright," the singer-songwriter Janelle Monáe and her label-mate Jidenna, a Nigerian American rapper, led a Black Lives Matter protest in Philadelphia, which was followed by a concert the next day. Monáe had written a track called "Hell You Talmbout" that became one of the anthems of the movement. In it, she chanted the names of Black Americans whose unjust deaths had moved activists to take a stand.

Onstage and off, Monáe reminded people that remembering and honoring those who had been killed was itself a form of activism. "Silence is our enemy, but sound is our weapon," she told the Philadelphia crowd. She urged the audience to join the chorus of reckoning: "Can we speak their names, as long as we have breath in our bodies?"

Monáe's song slowly picked up momentum in the years that followed—in 2019, the musician David Byrne performed a cover of it as the finale of every performance of his award-winning Broadway musical, *American Utopia*— and it took on new urgency during the 2020 protests. In

we still need that music to heal. And I think that 'Alright' is definitely one of those records that makes you feel good no matter what the times are."

interviews that summer, Monáe addressed white allies like Byrne, whom she saw as having important roles in the fight. "In the same ways that we have been marching, we have been screaming that Black Lives Matter, I'm asking of my white friends, or those who consider themselves supporters of me and us during this time, to have those conversations around white supremacy and around why your ancestors started chattel slavery," she urged a roundtable of actresses, most of them white, for *The Hollywood Reporter*. And those conversations, she said, needed to be followed by action: "This is a moment for Black people to stand our ground and ask more of our systems. Because it can't just be, 'We're going to march with you and do a hashtag'; it has to be rooted in justice as well. Systemic change has to be made."

(Top) Janelle Monáe, center in red, and Jidenna, center in white, march through Times Square at a rally to end mass incarceration in August 2015, where protesters joined them in singing "Hell You Talmbout."

(Bottom) In conjunction with the Black Lives Matter demonstrations in June 2020, the musician Jon Batiste performed a series of free concerts in New York, where he played his own reinvented version of "The Star-Spangled Banner." "The way that Jimi Hendrix took the song, the way that Marvin Gaye or Whitney took it–that tradition is what I am thinking of when I play it," he told *The New York Times*. "The diaspora that they infused into it is a response to the toxic ideologies that are embedded in the song and thus in the culture."

A THROWBACK PROTEST PLAYLIST

1. **"Strange Fruit,"** Billie Holiday

2. **"Mississippi Goddam,"** Nina Simone

3. **"A Change Is Gonna Come,"** Sam Cooke

4. **"What's Going On,"** Marvin Gaye

5. **"We Shall Overcome,"** Joan Baez

6. **"The Revolution Will Not Be Televised,"** Gil Scott-Heron

7. **"To Be Young, Gifted and Black,"** Donny Hathaway

8. **"Say It Loud: I'm Black and I'm Proud,"** James Brown

9. **"Freedom Highway,"** The Staple Singers

10. **"How I Got Over,"** Mahalia Jackson

11. **"The Times They Are a-Changin',"** Bob Dylan

12. **"Front Line,"** Stevie Wonder

13. **"Oh Freedom,"** Odetta

14. **"Water No Get Enemy,"** Fela Kuti

15. **"Wake Up Everybody,"** Harold Melvin and the Blue Notes

16. **"People Get Ready,"** The Impressions

17. **"O-o-h Child,"** The Five Stairsteps

18. **"Get Up, Stand Up,"** Bob Marley and the Wailers

19. **"Fight the Power,"** Public Enemy

20. **"Keep Ya Head Up,"** Tupac Shakur

A BLACK LIVES MATTER PLAYLIST

1. **"Alright,"** Kendrick Lamar

2. **"We the People,"** A Tribe Called Quest

3. **"Hell You Talmbout,"** Janelle Monáe

4. **"I Give You Power,"** Arcade Fire and Mavis Staples

5. **"This is America,"** Childish Gambino

6. **"Sandra's Smile,"** Blood Orange

7. **"Glory,"** Common, featuring John Legend

8. **"Baltimore,"** Prince, featuring Eryn Allen Kane

9. **"Black,"** Dave

10. **"Mad,"** Solange, featuring Lil Wayne

11. **"Rise Up,"** Andra Day

12. **"Nina Cried Power,"** Hozier, featuring Mavis Staples

13. **"I Can't Breathe,"** H.E.R.

14. **"Black Parade,"** Beyoncé

15. **"Freedom,"** Beyoncé and Kendrick Lamar

16. **"Lockdown,"** Anderson .Paak

17. **"The Charade,"** D'Angelo

18. **"Cops Shot the Kid,"** Nas, featuring Kanye West

19. **"Sweeter,"** Leon Bridges

20. **"I Just Want to Live,"** Keedron Bryant

2014 TO 2020

MURALS WITH A MESSAGE

In the summer of 1967, a group of artists known as the Organization of Black American Culture got together to create a tribute to Black heroes—a monument where people could gather to celebrate Black America.

They chose a building in Chicago as their canvas. For weeks, painters covered the two-story building with portraits—of activists like Malcolm X and W.E.B. Du Bois, of athletes like Muhammad Ali and Bill Russell, and of cultural icons like Aretha Franklin, Miles Davis, Cicely Tyson, and Nina Simone.

The *Wall of Respect* was dedicated on August 27, 1967. In the years that followed, portraits were added and removed. Tourists visited it, and community gatherings were held in its shadow. In 1971, the mural was lost to a fire, but its spirit lived on. According to the art historian Michael D. Harris, in the eight years after the *Wall* was created, more than fifteen hundred murals were painted in Black neighborhoods across the United States.

Murals have a long history as powerful tools for liberation movements around the world—from Mexico, where such artists as Diego Rivera and David Alfaro Siqueiros created tributes to the importance of everyday people in shaping the future of the nation; to Northern Ireland; to Communist East Germany. And that legacy continues today. Black Lives Matter murals can be found all over the United States, bridging past and present, joining the leaders of the civil rights movement with activists today.

In Minneapolis, artists began creating murals to honor George Floyd on the day he died. For months, tributes to him, Breonna Taylor, Ahmaud Arbery, and others continued to pop up across the country. These memorials become gathering places where the community can mourn and protest. And works of public art keep the history and values of the movement top of mind long after the crowds have dispersed.

From California to Kansas to Kentucky, here are some of those works.

Around 3:30 a.m. on June 5, 2020, a DC Department of Public Works crew began rolling out yellow paint on two blocks of Sixteenth Street across from Lafayette Square, a public park near the White House where, a few days earlier, peaceful protesters had been driven out by tear gas and riot police so that President Donald Trump could stage a photo op. In fifty-foot-tall letters, the workers painted BLACK LIVES MATTER, proclaiming not just the value of Black life but also the right of protesters to occupy this public space. "There was a dispute this week about whose street it is," Mayor Muriel Bowser's chief of staff, John Falcicchio, told reporters. "And Mayor Bowser wanted to make it abundantly clear whose street it is and honor the peaceful demonstrators who assembled."

This large-scale mural in Atlanta, Georgia, honors the late congressman John Lewis, who died in July 2020. It was produced by The Loss Prevention Arts, a collective whose mission is "to transform communities with art." The mural, part of their Hero series, includes a quote from the civil rights icon's speech at the 1963 March on Washington: "I appeal to all of you to get into this great revolution that is sweeping this nation. Get in and stay in the streets of every city, every village and hamlet of this nation until true freedom comes, until the revolution of 1776 is complete."

To celebrate Juneteenth 2020, the artists Menace Two and Resa Piece wanted to honor two key figures from the civil rights movement: Malcolm X and Martin Luther King. The two men *"had polarizing political views, but their intention was the same–to empower and equalize black people of this country,"* the artists wrote in an Instagram post unveiling the Williamsburg, Brooklyn, mural. *"Let's continue their legacy and fight for equality by upholding the values and wisdom that these men embodied. We can have more peace if we have more justice in this system."*

Murals have become a common way to honor victims of police brutality and gun violence, serving as both a lasting public tribute to those who have been lost and a gathering place for the community to mourn. This one in Louisville, Kentucky, features portraits of Breonna Taylor, George Floyd, and others—including David McAtee, a fifty-three-year-old Louisville barbecue restaurant owner who was shot and killed by a National Guard soldier in June 2020 while protesting Taylor's death. It took three artists—Braylyn Stewart, Whitney Holbourn, and Andrew Norris—about two weeks to complete the mural. At its unveiling in July, Stewart thanked the community for supporting their work. "To give this as a gift to the city and have it last and stand there is something that is beyond words," he said.

This mural in Minneapolis honoring George Floyd became a makeshift memorial, with community members coming to pay their respects to the former high school football star, hip-hop artist, and dad. "When you look at the piece, the first thing that hits you is the brightness of those colors, which allows you to be reflective, but also celebrate a person," said the artist Cadex Herrera, who produced the tribute along with Xena Goldman, Greta McLain, and others. "I'm very touched that the mural has become a symbol: a place to heal and reflect and think about your place in George Floyd's life."

The artist Anita Easterwood created this painting–titled "I Will"–in Kansas City, Kansas, with her father, the muralist Rodney "Lucky" Easterwood, in the wake of the killing of George Floyd. It was inspired by a piece by a young poet named Justice Davis, Anita said, which reads in part, "Momma, You don't have to cry. / I will not let them steal my joy; I've hid it behind my fist raised to the sky. / I will fly without limit, like my dreams are waiting for me on the other side of the horizon." Anita told *The Pitch* that, in their mural, she and her dad chose not to show the child's face "because we wanted anybody, any young Black kid in that area to be able to resonate with that image."

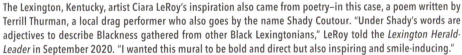

The Lexington, Kentucky, artist Ciara LeRoy's inspiration also came from poetry–in this case, a poem written by Terrill Thurman, a local drag performer who also goes by the name Shady Coutour. "Under Shady's words are adjectives to describe Blackness gathered from other Black Lexingtonians," LeRoy told the *Lexington Herald-Leader* in September 2020. "I wanted this mural to be bold and direct but also inspiring and smile-inducing."

Camila Ibarra, a civil engineering student at Arizona State University, was part of a group of artists who painted Black Lives Matter murals around downtown Tucson, Arizona, in the summer of 2020. *"I couldn't stand to sit around and simply retweet. I had to do something,"* she wrote in an Instagram post about her piece, which she also printed on posters and T-shirts that she sold to raise money for organizations supporting the movement. *"This is my protest. This is my support for the black community. I am here for you. I love you."*

We want
Education
For Our People
that Exposes
the true nature
of this decadent

American Society
We want
Education
that teaches us
our true history
and role in Present Time
– Black Panther Party

ITS NOT ABOUT
SUPPLICATION
ITS ABOUT POWER
ITS NOT
ABOUT ASKING
ITS ABOUT
DEMANDING

ITS NOT ABOUT
CONVINCING THOSE
WHO ARE CURRENTLY
IN POWER ITS ABOUT CHANGING THE VERY
FACE OF POWER ITSELF

BLACK
LIVES

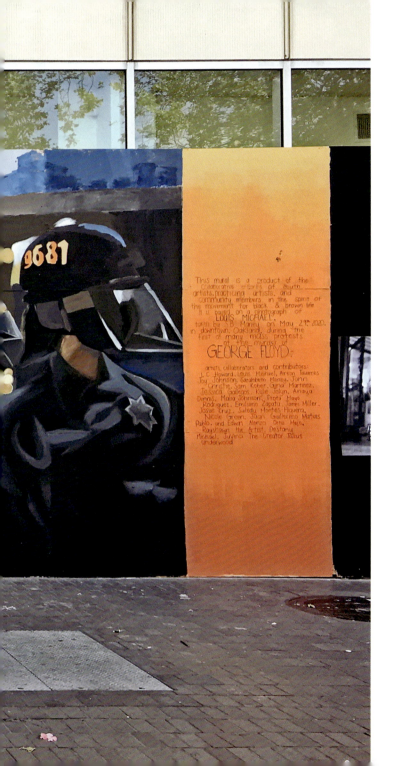

The Oakland Super Heroes Mural Project took Sarahbeth Maney's photograph of Louis Michael at a Black Lives Matter protest and transformed it into this painting, which they titled *Turning Anger into Action*. Michael had just finished college, but his graduation ceremony was canceled because of the coronavirus pandemic. So he wore his cap and gown to the demonstration, carrying a cardboard sign. YOUNG BLACK COLLEGE GRAD, it read. WHICH PART IS THREATENING? The image of him with his fist in the air came to symbolize a generation of young people galvanized by this movement. "I was trying to make a statement of what it's like to be a Black graduate in 2020," Michael told the news station *KRON*. "I was feeling empowered standing in front of the police with my fist up. I knew I was making a statement."

A group of kids decorate T-shirts at a memorial to George Floyd in Minneapolis on June 4, 2020.

CHAPTER 8

THE ART OF PROTEST

A movement gets its message across in many ways. The gathering of individuals, en masse, to stand together and march in the same direction makes a powerful statement about the people's support for a cause. Chants and songs communicate their common goals to all who can hear. And another one of the most powerful ways that a movement grows and spreads is through visual art. Murals, signs, paintings, and installations give a movement its distinctive style and spread the word about its mission.

At any protest there will almost certainly be a sea of signs floating above the people. These signs are so much more than words lettered on a piece of cardboard or plywood. They are each like brushstrokes that come together with hundreds of thousands—even millions—of others to form a portrait of a movement for change.

The use of signs to rally a movement stretches back through American history. In 1913, on the day before President Woodrow Wilson's inauguration, the National American Woman Suffrage Association organized a march through Washington, DC, to protest the denial of women's right to vote. It was, at the time, the largest demonstration the nation's capital had ever seen. Thousands of people participated—far more than attended the inauguration—including the journalist and antilynching crusader Ida B. Wells-Barnett. And as the suffragists marched, they carried banners and signs that expressed their support for the cause. A few years after the march, a group of suffragists from the National Woman's Party staged a protest outside the White House. They were known as the Silent Sentinels because they did not speak as they stood outside, six days a week, in all kinds of weather. Instead, they carried signs that did the talking for them. MR. PRESIDENT, one banner demanded, HOW LONG MUST WOMEN WAIT FOR LIBERTY?

Almost half a century later, civil rights activists took to the streets of the capital for the 1963 March on Washington. An individual voice can't make itself heard in the din of a crowd of hundreds of thousands, but with their signs, protesters then and now have spoken out, loud and clear, about what moved them to march. In 2020, there were signs that declared,

WE ARE MARCHING FOR FREEDOM, OURS AND YOURS
NO JUSTICE, NO PEACE
WHITE SILENCE = BLACK DEATH
WE DIDN'T COME THIS FAR TO ONLY COME THIS FAR.

And some of them echoed the language of those who had marched before:

WE DEMAND AN END TO POLICE BRUTALITY NOW!

At protests today, from the Women's March to the

Demonstrators outside the Lincoln Memorial during the March on Washington for Jobs and Freedom on August 29, 1963.

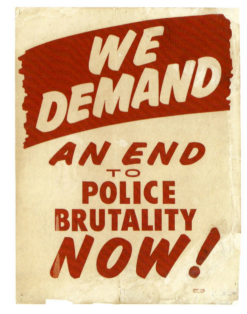

The art historian Samuel Y. Edgerton donated this poster, which he carried at the March on Washington, to the Smithsonian's National Museum of African American History and Culture. "The message after fifty years is still unresolved," he told Smithsonian magazine in 2017.

March for Our Lives to climate strikes and demonstrations for Black Lives Matter, signs continue to make demonstrators' messages heard. Some are straightforward. Others are clever, using wordplay, pop culture references, or even memes to make their point. Some focus on text while others bloom with illustrations and graphic design. At the 2017 Women's March, the comedian and writer Lauren Brown saw her tweets repurposed on signs throughout the crowds. She was flattered, even honored, that her words had resonated with so many people with whom she was joined in a common cause. "Making a sign and showing up to a protest is an act of saying that you matter and your voice should be heard," she told *Vice*. "I don't think it matters if it's funny or original or not: it just matters that you're there saying it."

And it's not just about what a sign says. Signs can also be a way of creating a visual language of a movement. And sometimes an image, especially one that is held up and

Protesters at a June 2020 rally for Black Lives Matter outside the Stonewall Inn in New York, which is widely considered the birthplace of the gay rights movement in the United States. The imagery and language on their banners evoke posters carried by gay rights activists in the 1980s: groups such as the AIDS Coalition to Unleash Power, better known as ACT UP, used pink triangles and the phrase "Silence = Death" when protesting the government's inaction during the AIDS epidemic that killed more than six hundred thousand Americans—the majority of whom were members of the LGBTQIA+ community, and a disproportionate number of whom were people of color.

Hundreds of protesters carrying homemade signs march through Columbia, South Carolina, on May 30, 2020, to demand justice for George Floyd.

amplified across a march, can speak louder than any words. "We aren't born woke. Something wakes us up," DeRay Mckesson explained to *Pitchfork*. "For some people, that's a video of police violence, or their proximity to a friend, or a protest. For some people, it's art."

Artists, both amateur and professional, have long used their talents to advocate for issues they care about. And they have done it on scales both large and small, from the pavement to the sky.

In June 2020, in the wake of the killing of George Floyd, the rallying cry "Black Lives Matter" was splashed across blacktops and fences, walls and telephone poles, by individual artists and community groups. Murals were a way for these communities to come together and proclaim

their support for the movement for racial justice. They started as homegrown works of art, many scrawled in sidewalk chalk or spray paint, but they quickly grew in scale. And official entities jumped on the bandwagon, too. Just as the DC Department of Public Works had painted BLACK LIVES MATTER on the street leading to the White House, similar street murals appeared across the country, from California to Colorado to Florida. In Oak Park, Illinois, a group of students and recent college graduates painted one on Scoville Avenue, in a historically Black neighborhood just outside Chicago. In New York City, Mayor Bill de Blasio did the same on Fifth Avenue. He was joined by the Central Park Five, a group of Black men who were wrongfully imprisoned as teenagers and spent six to thirteen years in prison for a crime they did not commit. The mural was painted outside Trump Tower, the landmark real estate holding and former home of President Donald Trump, who in 1989 had publicly called for the five to be executed, even after evidence emerged that they were not responsible for the crime of which they were accused.

These days, artists don't always need expanses of pavement to make their mark. Instagram and other social media platforms have helped them take their work from the street to the world. In 2013, as Black Lives Matter was first emerging, Nikkolas Smith, a concept artist, children's book author, and film illustrator, began a series he called "Sunday Sketches." He drew portraits of the victims the movement honored, depicting them with respect and joy and grace. The images, he wrote in *Time* magazine, were a way for him "to pull myself out of a dark place."

In the same way that #BlackLivesMatter had grown and spread, the images soon caught the world's attention. Other activists shared them; politicians and celebrities amplified them even further. Smith began seeing his art all over the place—not just on social media but on protest signs carried in marches around the world.

Smith sees a natural link between art and activism. "There are so many problems and issues in the world, sometimes you wish you could just grab everybody and direct them toward solutions. Putting those issues into words isn't that easy for me," he wrote in *Time*. "But art innately has the ability to move people: to shout out, 'This is wrong! This needs to be fixed!' in a matter of seconds. People are able to rally around even just a single image. It's my job to get their attention and then show them how they can create some sort of positive change."

In the summer of 2020, the Black Lives Matter Global Network Foundation asked Smith to create a portrait of George Floyd. They chose him, they said, because of the dignity with which he honored his subjects' lives. Kailee Scales, the foundation's managing director, told *NPR* that "Nikkolas is one of those artists who call on us to change the way we see ourselves." Smith's portrait was striking because it featured Floyd in a tuxedo, with the words "Justice for George" in faint, whitish gray letters on either side of him. As Smith later explained, "I found an image of George Floyd in a black hoodie, and thought that was a good base reference to begin with, but in my re-creation tribute, I wanted to suit him up with a tuxedo and focus his eyes directly at the viewer."

"YOU HAVE A POWERFUL TOOL TO PAINT THE WORLD YOU WANT TO SEE. SOMETIMES, THAT MEANS PAINTING THE BROKEN THINGS TO WAKE PEOPLE UP."

— Nikkolas Smith

Smith made similar portraits of Ahmaud Arbery and Breonna Taylor. All three portraits were done with rough, unfinished brushstrokes—symbolic, Smith said, of their unfinished lives.

When he posted Floyd's portrait on Instagram, Smith wrote, *"Black lives in this country are being destroyed by a virus of racism, fear and hatred. It is up to everyone to take a stand and actively work to tear down this centuries-old pandemic. NOW."* Black Lives Matter took his message and amplified it even further, putting the portrait on billboards in Los Angeles, Atlanta, and New York's Times Square.

Works like Smith's do more than just broadcast the message of the Black Lives Matter movement: they remind viewers that these were real people whose lives ended too soon, not just another statistic. Peter Sellars, a professor at UCLA who teaches art as social and moral action, told *NPR,* "It's keeping memory alive, and memory is frequently what gives you a level of courage that's more than you think you have because, in fact, you're not alone."

It's not a responsibility that Smith takes lightly. But it's work he feels he needs to do, especially now that he has become a father, shepherding a new generation into an uncertain and often scary world. "For young artists, I always try to remind them: you have a powerful tool to paint the world you want to see," he wrote in *Time*. "Sometimes, that means painting the broken things to wake people up."

It is that unique power of art—to make stark and unavoidable the things people don't want to look at—that

Nikkolas Smith's portraits of, from left, George Floyd, Breonna Taylor, and Ahmaud Arbery. "A lot of my pieces are unfinished," Smith told *NPR* in 2020. "I feel like that kind of is a parallel to these people's lives because they did not get a chance to really finish their life like they should have."

makes it such a powerful tool of protest. Jammie Holmes, a painter from Louisiana, created what he called an aerial demonstration in response to George Floyd's killing. On May 30, 2020, planes flew banners over five cities across the United States. Each banner represented some of Floyd's final words. Holmes sought to connect "these places across the United States to support Minneapolis in a national protest against police brutality within the African American community."

The banner that flew over Detroit read PLEASE I CAN'T BREATHE.

Over Miami, the banner read MY STOMACH HURTS.

High above the city of Dallas, the words were MY NECK HURTS.

A plane flew through a cloudy Los Angeles sky, reading EVERYTHING HURTS.

And finally, in New York, there was a banner that sent chills through everyone who looked up and saw it: THEY'RE GOING TO KILL ME.

A banner from Jammie Holmes's immersive art piece "They're Going to Kill Me" flies over New York City on May 30, 2020. In his artist's statement, Holmes described the aerial demonstration as "an act of social conscience and protest meant to bring people together in their shared incense at the inhumane treatment of American citizens."

WHO'S WHO AT A PROTEST

In the wake of the killings of George Floyd, Breonna Taylor, and Ahmaud Arbery, a nation rose to its feet to say, "Enough is enough." Although the Black Lives Matter marches hit their peak on June 6, 2020, in many cities such as New York near-daily demonstrations continued for weeks, or even months. Organizers developed a playbook for how to successfully plan and execute a smooth and effective protest. They learned to handle everything from traffic to dehydration to directing large crowds. They developed strategies for keeping protesters safe, even amid a pandemic and when dealing with physical confrontations with police. And they designed clearly defined roles, drawing on different people's skills to keep marches on track from start to finish. Here's a breakdown of what those roles look like.

Based on the story "From Bike Blockers to Street Medics: The Anatomy of an N.Y.C. Protest" by Juliana Kim, with photographs by Simbarashe Cha, published in *The New York Times* on September 19, 2020, and on the accompanying Instagram story, produced by Lily Benson.

MARSHALS

- Help maintain momentum
- Scattered across the march to help guide protesters
- Often wearing safety vests and carrying bullhorns

Larry Malcolm Smith Jr. began protesting at age eight after Sean Bell, a Black man in his neighborhood, was shot and killed by police. As a marshal, he is there to make sure that the protest runs smoothly. "I don't feel like I chose activism," he told *The New York Times*. "Activism chose me."

BIKE PATROL

- Cyclists clear the streets ahead of the march
- Work to de-escalate tensions when they meet uncooperative motorists
- Scout for new routes when marches go off course

Brandon English, a visual artist, grew up in Cobb County, Georgia, where white drivers used to heckle and even verbally threaten him on his way home from school. So he wasn't fazed by the potential danger of being the first line of defense against motorists during a march. "That's something that's been understood for me as a Black person in the United States," he told *The Times*. "Whether I'm protesting or not, my life can be in danger."

THE FRONTLINE

- Protesters who are willing to risk arrest or injury
- Sometimes form a physical line of defense against police officers

Frontline protesters face a line of police at a Black Lives Matter rally in Union Square in New York on May 28, 2020.

STREET MEDICS

- Help with potential injuries or assist protesters who are feeling unwell
- Carry backpacks, usually marked with red crosses, stuffed with first-aid supplies
- Keep saline solution on hand in case of mace or tear gas exposure

A medic watches as a group of protesters begins to gather for a Black Lives Matter demonstration in Washington Square Park in New York on June 8, 2020.

SUPPLIERS

- Carry water, snacks, hand sanitizer, masks, and hygiene products in case protesters need them
- Get the marchers what they need so they can keep going

Kevin Mora, a lab technician from Connecticut, joined the protests in New York as a street medic in May 2020 but soon realized that there was an urgent need for more suppliers. He started Your Fight Too, a mobile bodega that provides everything from masks to food. Mora, who is Ecuadorian and bisexual, told *The Times* that he used to be more concerned with how others were being allies for him. But the demonstrations in 2020 made him ask himself, "How have I been an ally in return?"

LEGAL OBSERVERS

- Act as witnesses
- Document interactions between protesters and police, including arrests or potential civil rights violations
- Connect protesters to legal representation and help those who are arrested

Erica Johnson is a brand manager at a marketing company but has been volunteering with the National Lawyers Guild as a legal observer, documenting interactions between protesters and police, for nearly a decade. "Especially when it's my own community, I feel like I have to show up a lot more," she told *The Times*. "I feel like I can't do enough."

A Black Lives Matter sit-in in Piedmont Park in Atlanta on June 19, 2020.

CHAPTER 9

WHAT PEOPLE POWER CAN DO

By the summer of 2020, Black Lives Matter had become a global movement. Thousands of groups representing millions of people were aligned with the cause. The social media campaign that began with a single post on Facebook had grown so big that on May 28, as people responded to the killing of George Floyd, more than eight million tweets tagged #BlackLivesMatter were posted on Twitter. (In contrast, just six years earlier, after the death of Eric Garner, the number of tweets with this hashtag numbered fewer than 150,000.) Where previous protests had drawn hundreds or maybe occasionally thousands of people, in 2020, over the course of just a few months, more than fifteen million Americans poured into the streets to stand up for Black lives, likely making it the largest protest movement in the nation's history. And in cities all over the globe, thousands more stood and marched in solidarity with them, chanting Floyd's name and demanding change. Finally, after years of painstakingly slow progress, it seemed that things were starting to shift.

"Alicia, Opal, and I created a container for Black protest to be seen and taken seriously," Patrisse Cullors told *Time* magazine that September. "And then just like dandelions, folks bloomed out of that. And so we can't take sole responsibility for 3,000 protests around the globe, because that's people listening, and responding, and saying, 'OK, we hear the words "Black Lives Matter." We're going to prove it. We're going to take it to the streets.'"

The 2020 protests did not emerge out of nowhere. The frustration, anger, and determination that fueled them had been building for years, not just within Black Lives Matter but in a wave of demonstrations that occurred across the United States after the election of President Donald Trump. This progressive movement began the day after Trump's inauguration, with the Women's March of 2017, and grew in response to his administration's policies, from rallies at airports in January 2017 to protest the Muslim travel ban, to demonstrations against the family separation policy at the Mexican-American border in 2018, to numerous marches calling for government action on climate change, health care, and gun violence. "The bonds among these movements and the organizations that coordinate them are fragile," the sociologist Dana R. Fisher writes in her book *American Resistance: From the Women's March to the Blue Wave*. But together they were able to reach many Americans who had not previously been engaged in politics, progressive or otherwise. People are no longer living in their own bubbles, Fisher writes. "They are marching, yelling, and working together."

Still, at no point had these demonstrations turned out the massive numbers of people that the Black Lives Matter protests drew in 2020. So what made that spring different? For starters, there was a pandemic. By late May, a new coronavirus had, in the span of a few short months, been the cause of one hundred thousand deaths in the United States—a number that was shocking and hard to fully take in, and which would only continue to grow in the months

Thousands of health care workers, many of them wearing their scrubs and lab coats, gathered for a Black Lives Matter demonstration in Seattle on June 6, 2020. As they marched from a public hospital to City Hall, they carried signs that read BLACK HEALTH MATTERS and RACISM IS A PUBLIC HEALTH EMERGENCY.

to come. Many compared the loss of life with the death toll of wars. In fact, the fatalities were more than double the number of U.S. soldiers killed in combat during the entire Vietnam War. But the Vietnam War lasted a decade. To lose so many lives so quickly was hard to bear. Thousands of Americans also lost their jobs because of the pandemic, leading to the highest rate of unemployment in nearly a century. This added to a feeling of unease and defenselessness that crossed racial, gender, and economic lines.

And Black Americans were much more likely to be affected by both of these crises than white Americans. People of color, and especially Black people, were more likely to experience serious illness or to die from Covid-19, according to Dr. Sherita Golden, the chief diversity officer at Johns Hopkins University School of Medicine. In Milwaukee, Wisconsin, for example, Black people made up 26 percent of the county population and 70 percent of deaths from the pandemic. One study in early June found that Black Americans across the country were dying at two and a half times the rate of white Americans. And Black Americans, who were less likely to be able to work remotely, more likely to be essential workers, and less likely to have substantial savings to live off of than white Americans, were also disproportionately affected by the economic crisis that came in the pandemic's wake. It was a vicious conundrum: people couldn't afford to stay home and risk losing their jobs and income, which in turn made them much more likely to be exposed to the virus and get sick.

"The pandemic added its own accelerant to the mix," the writer Jenna Wortham explained in *The New York Times.* "For roughly three months before Mr. Floyd's death, Americans were living in a state of hypervigilance and anxiety, coping with feelings of uncertainty, fear, and vulnerability—things many black Americans experience on a regular basis."

Perhaps that shared trauma, along with empathy, was what moved so many more Americans than ever before to get involved. With many previous tragedies, the grief of families and communities had been expressed in vigils and largely local protests that only sometimes made national news. But this moment was different. Part of it too was that people were responding not just to the murder of George Floyd but also to the killings of Ahmaud Arbery and Breonna Taylor. These three losses, coming in the span of a few months and amid such immense national trauma, created a uniquely pressurized moment that seemed to hit home with people in a new way.

The protests of 2020 were striking not just in their scale but also in their diversity, reflecting a shift in the national consciousness. In 2015, only half of all Americans considered racial discrimination "a big problem." By June 2020, according to a Monmouth University poll, that number had jumped to 76 percent. Pictures and videos of the protests that year showed people of all races, genders, and ages marching together. And as more and more people saw more and more people standing up and speaking out, they felt compelled to do the same.

The diversity of the movement's support did not surprise its founders, whose goal from the beginning was to appeal to the shared humanity of all Americans. "One thing I'm very clear about is that there's so much we have in common," said Alicia Garza. "We all want to live lives where we feel safe, where we are able to live with dignity, and where we're connected."

In early 2020, a study by the online survey research firm Civiqs found that around 40 percent of American voters supported Black Lives Matter. That support had been building incrementally since the movement first emerged in 2013; in April 2017, when Civiqs first started studying it, 37 percent of people said they supported the cause. But in late May and early June 2020, as protests took hold across the country and around the globe, that number skyrocketed, increasing almost as much in two weeks as it had in the preceding two years. An estimated fifteen to twenty-six million Americans took to the streets to march for Black Lives Matter over those transformative weeks. By June 10, the number of voters who supported the movement had risen to 52 percent.

This level of widespread support was hard to imagine when Black Lives Matter first started as a conversation between three friends. Throughout the movement's history it has faced consistent and significant backlash. With campaigns like #BlueLivesMatter, which was coined in support of the police, and #AllLivesMatter, people dismissed the activists' core claim that racism was a persistent problem that endangered the lives of Black people in the United States. The majority of the 2020 protests were peaceful, but there were some scattered incidents of looting and vandalism, and as a result, a significant number of Americans came to oppose the movement, even as majority support rose.

Black Lives Matter's success in shifting public opinion seems to follow what social scientists call the "contact hypothesis," which they have studied in other social justice movements. The more examples individual people see of a marginalized group or cause, and the more personal conversations they have with people in their own life about these issues, the more likely public opinion is to shift. Talking to a family member, friend, or neighbor may seem like a small act, but studies have found that these conversations can have a dramatic, cumulative effect on the national dialogue. Another example of this is the movement to expand

A government employee installs a street sign officially designating a stretch of 16th Street NW in Washington, DC, as Black Lives Matter Plaza on June 5, 2020. Mayor Muriel Bowser also commissioned a Black Lives Matter street mural to mark the plaza, which faces Lafayette Square and the White House.

rights for LGBTQIA+ people. In 2004, Pew Research Center polls showed that the majority of Americans—60 percent—opposed legalizing same-sex marriage, while only 31 percent were in favor. By 2019, those numbers had been reversed, with 61 percent of Americans supporting same-sex marriage and only 31 percent opposing it. A huge part of that shift, experts say, was thanks to greater visibility of LGBTQIA+ people, from marches and protests and media coverage to pop culture.

Changing minds is slow, often dispiriting work. As the reporter John Eligon wrote in *The New York Times,* "Along with the long hours, constant confrontation and frequent heartbreak they experience, activists work for little or no pay and sometimes struggle for basic needs like food and shelter even as they push for societal change." Finding ways to take care of themselves—mentally, emotionally, and physically—has become an essential conversation among young activists today. Change takes time. On a personal level, the people who are working on the front lines need to find ways to sustain themselves in order to go the distance—whether it's meditation, therapy, or even just taking a break. And on an organizational level, challenges of transparency, scale, and financial management also often come up as groups like the Black Lives Matter Global Network Foundation rapidly expand.

Progress isn't a straight line, but hope is the engine that keeps movements alive. In 2013, the same year Black Lives Matter was born, the Supreme Court justice Ruth Bader Ginsburg took Martin Luther King's words about the arc of the moral universe a step further. Yes, she wrote, that arc does bend toward justice—but only if there is "a steadfast national commitment to see the task through to completion."

And of course, protest isn't just about changing hearts and minds. It's about turning that change into action.

In August 2016, a few years after that pivotal summer in Ferguson, a group of activists called the Movement for Black Lives (M4BL) launched "A Vision for Black Lives,"

Black Lives Matter activists protest in Brooklyn on May 29, 2020–four days after the killing of George Floyd by a white Minneapolis police offer.

which outlined their proposals for transforming the criminal justice system, rooting out systemic racism, and stemming the tide of violence and death that affected the Black community. Their platform included six main areas of policy: ending the violence inflicted on Black people, including by law enforcement and through mass incarceration; reparations to compensate Black Americans for the harm done to them by the government and other institutions; shifting money from prisons and police to invest in education, health care, and public safety for these communities; economic empowerment for Black Americans; changes to give them a more powerful voice in the political system; and community oversight of police to ensure that wrongdoing was properly investigated, documented, made public, and met with repercussions that would prevent it from happening again.

Groups like Campaign Zero, cofounded by DeRay Mckesson, Johnetta Elzie, Brittany Packnett Cunningham, and Samuel Sinyangwe, worked to translate these ideas into concrete policy recommendations, blending research and community feedback with input from groups like President Barack Obama's policing task force. They made some progress. In 2016, for example, Newark, New Jersey, which had a long history of conflict between its Black residents and police, established a civilian review board to look into claims of wrongdoing or racial bias by law enforcement, and cities across the nation began to require police officers to wear body cameras so that incidents of violence were documented and could be properly investigated. But there was still a long way to go.

In 2020, as public opinion swelled in their favor, Black Lives Matter organizers set to work harnessing that momentum for change. They took advantage of the moment to listen to what communities were saying and to reimagine their goals. On June 19, 2020—a holiday known as Juneteenth, which marks the day in 1865 when the last enslaved African Americans in the United States were told that they had been released from bondage by the Emancipation Proclamation—M4BL relaunched its "Vision for Black Lives." The six-point platform was expanded to thirteen different planks, and there were now specific provisions that spoke to the needs of Black women, of Black migrants, of Black disabled people, of Black members of the LGBTQIA+ community. "We demand nothing short of liberation," the collective wrote.

Across the nation, many of their demands were being expressed and amplified by protesters in the streets. In chants and on signs and across social media, people called out for the elevation of marginalized Black voices and the protection of those who, like Black trans women, were among the most vulnerable in the community. And one slogan in

Tiffany Munroe, a Black trans activist from Guyana, waves a pride flag at Brooklyn Liberation–a rally for Black trans lives held on June 14, 2020. Demonstrators wore all white as they silently marched through the borough from Grand Army Plaza to Fort Greene Park.

particular, which summed up many of Black Lives Matter's demands, began to grow in popularity: "Defund the police." As explained in Chapter 4, this phrase encompasses a wide range of proposals but essentially boils down to one core directive: governments should make communities safer by shifting money away from police departments, which often take up an outsize percentage of a city's budget, and redistributing those resources to such areas as mental health services, education, housing, and health care. This reimagining of public safety, activists argue, would actually do more to combat crime and violence by addressing not just the issues themselves but also the systemic problems at their root.

In a matter of months, advocates for defunding began to see signs of progress across the nation. On June 3 in Los Angeles, Mayor Eric Garcetti called for $100 million to $150 million in cuts to the police budget. On June 7 in New York,

Mayor Bill de Blasio called for legislators to take $1 *billion* out of the New York City Police Department's $6 billion budget and move it to youth and social services. But the biggest change came in Minneapolis, where, on June 7, the city council vowed to dismantle and remake the city's police department. Their statement read, in part: "Decades of police reform efforts have proved that the Minneapolis Police Department cannot be reformed and will never be accountable for its actions. We are here today to begin the process of ending the Minneapolis police department and creating a new transformative model for cultivating safety in Minneapolis."

The ripple effects of the Black Lives Matter protests spread far beyond the borders of the United States. In the fall, young activists in Nigeria turned out en masse to call for the dismantling of the country's Special Anti-Robbery Squad, a police unit with a history of abuse and human rights violations. The wave of protests began in early October in the capital of Lagos and quickly spread to more than twenty other cities across the country. Much like Black Lives Matter, the #EndSARS movement, which had been building for years, was fueled by incidents of police brutality that were caught on video, and the young people at its forefront used social media to organize protests and spread the word about their cause. And, also like Black Lives Matter, the Nigerian protests were met with a militant response from law enforcement. More than fifteen hundred people were arrested during or after the protests, and many organizers' bank accounts were frozen as the government tried to control the uprising. And at one protest in Lekki, a suburb of Lagos, soldiers opened fire on a crowd of peaceful protesters, killing at least ten.

The conversation about racial justice and policing in the United States in 2020 also had an effect on that year's elections. While voters were divided on how they felt about the issue, they agreed almost universally that it was important. According to one survey conducted for the Associated Press, roughly 90 percent of voters said that the 2020 protests over police violence affected how they cast their ballots, with more than 75 percent of them saying it was a major factor in their decision and nearly 20 percent calling it the single most important issue. In races across the country, mayors, city council members, district attorneys, and other officials who had expressed support for many of Black Lives Matter's policies were victorious. And at the national level, Joe Biden, who promised to make rooting out systemic racism a top priority, defeated Donald Trump—who had referred to Black Lives Matter protesters as "thugs" and "terrorists"—in the November 2020 presidential election.

In some places, the consequences of those races were immediately apparent. In Los Angeles, for example, voters elected a progressive candidate, George Gascón, to be the county's new district attorney. At his swearing-in on December 7, he announced a slew of changes aimed at reducing incarceration rates and reforming the area's criminal justice system. This included ending cash bail, a system in which people charged with crimes, even nonviolent ones, must pay the court a sum of money in order to leave jail while they await trial. In many cases, this means that poorer offenders—many of whom are Black—end up spending time in jail without having been convicted of any crimes, simply because they cannot afford to leave. Abolishing cash bail has

A Black Lives Matter protester at a demonstration in the St. Louis suburb of St. Charles, Missouri, on June 6, 2020. More than 75 percent of American voters said the summer's uprisings influenced how they cast their ballots that fall.

long been a goal of Black Lives Matter and other progressive groups, who say the practice is discriminatory. And Gascón agreed. "How much money you have in your bank account is a terrible proxy for how dangerous you are," he said. "Today there are hundreds of people languishing in jails, not because they represent a danger to our community, but because they can't afford to purchase their freedom." The cash bail ban in Los Angeles County took effect on January 1, 2021.

Still, the path to making the systemic changes Black Lives Matter is fighting for is long, hard, and complicated. Many of the measures proposed in 2020 have already run into significant roadblocks. Some lawmakers who made sweeping promises in the heat of summer have started to backtrack, and proposals to reshape public safety in many major cities have collapsed or stalled. In Minneapolis, one of the city council members who joined the unanimous vote for defunding in June told *The New York Times* in September that he supported the measure "in spirit," but that putting it into action was another matter. The city's mayor has since come out against the proposal, and public opinion polls have turned against it, too. And that shift isn't unique to Minnesota: although many adults in the United States still say they support Black Lives Matter, that share had fallen to 48 percent three months after the peak of the protests.

But activists remain committed to seeing the reforms through. Floyd's death "did not simply start a bunch of good speeches, a bunch of tributes," the Reverend William Lawson, pastor emeritus at Wheeler Avenue Baptist Church in Houston, said during Floyd's funeral service. "Out of his death has come a movement. A worldwide movement. And that movement is not going to stop after two weeks, three weeks, a month. That movement is going to change the world."

In January 2021, the Olof Palme Memorial Fund announced that it was awarding its prestigious annual prize—given to a person or organization that has advanced the cause of human rights—to the Black Lives Matter Global Network Foundation. The Swedish foundation chose to honor Black Lives Matter, they said, for working for "peaceful civil disobedience against police brutality and racial violence all over the world." And on the same day the Olof Prize was announced, Petter Eide, a Norwegian official, revealed that he had nominated the movement for the Nobel Peace Prize.

"Awarding the peace prize to Black Lives Matter, as the strongest global force against racial injustice, will send a powerful message that peace is founded on equality, solidarity, and human rights," he wrote in his nomination. "And that all countries must respect those basic principles."

Tiana Day, seventeen, leads thousands of protesters in a Black Lives Matter march across the Golden Gate Bridge in San Francisco on June 6, 2020.

CHAPTER 10

NEVER TOO YOUNG TO LEAD

On Monday, February 1, 1960, the civil rights movement was forever changed when four Black students at North Carolina Agricultural and Technical State University—Ezell Blair Jr., eighteen; Franklin McCain, nineteen; Joseph McNeil, seventeen; and David Richmond, eighteen—took their seats at a Woolworth's lunch counter in Greensboro, North Carolina. They were dressed in their best clothes, collars perfectly starched, ties knotted with precision. Their hearts were racing as they felt all eyes turn to them. As they climbed onto the vinyl stools, they steeled themselves for the outrage, scorn, humiliation, and violence that could come. But they also knew they were doing their part to take a stand against the injustice of segregation, which they could no longer tolerate. "Almost instantaneously, after sitting down on a simple, dumb stool, I felt so

relieved," McCain told *Smithsonian* magazine years later. "I felt so clean, and I felt as though I had gained a little bit of my manhood by that simple act."

The store fell silent as the freshmen politely refused the increasingly agitated demands by first the waiter, then the manager, that they give up their seats. Store policy, as they well knew, forbade Black customers from sitting at the counter; if they wanted to order food, they had to take it to go. But the students would not budge. A policeman showed up, threatening them with his billy club. He paced back and forth behind them, but the four remained calmly in their seats. Eventually he gave up and left. Only when the manager announced that the store was closing early did Blair, McCain, McNeil, and Richmond leave their stools. A photographer snapped a photo of them before they left,

Activists stage a sit-in to protest the segregation of a lunch counter in Greensboro, North Carolina, in February 1960.

which caught the attention of the press. The next day, when they came back, about a dozen more people showed up to sit with them. Three days later the number had swelled to the hundreds—many of them high school and college students.

The Greensboro Four were not the first to stage a sit-in to end segregation—Diane Nash, John Lewis, and other members of the Nashville Student Movement, for example, had organized a similar campaign in Tennessee the year before—but theirs was the protest that really took off. The sit-ins continued into the summer, by which point they had spread to more than fifty cities across the country as other young activists were inspired by the work of the Greensboro

Four. One of these activists was Lewis. "Greensboro became the message," he said in a 2017 documentary for the History Channel. "If they can do it in Greensboro, we too can do it." On July 25, 1960, their efforts earned results. The Greensboro Woolworth's officially served its first Black customers. Other dining establishments across the region followed suit.

Just a few years after the Greensboro sit-ins, as the nation continued working to unravel the system of segregation that had strangled American society for decades, student-led protests shone a spotlight on the need for equity in the country's schools. On October 12, 1963, more than two hundred thousand students in Chicago—about half of the students in the city's school district—staged a one-day boycott, which they called Freedom Day. About twenty thousand of them marched to the Chicago Board of Education to demand equitable resources for Black students. The next year, more than 450,000 Black and Puerto Rican students led a similar boycott to protest racial inequality in New York's public schools. Thousands of demonstrators joined the peaceful rallies outside the New York City Board of Education, City Hall, and Governor Nelson Rockefeller's office in Manhattan.

In the 1970s and '80s, young people were at the forefront of the fight against apartheid, the system of racial segregation in South Africa. On June 16, 1976, thousands of students in Soweto, a Black township section of the city of Johannesburg, organized a march to protest a law mandating that all public education be conducted in Afrikaans, the language of the country's white citizens. What started as a peaceful protest soon turned violent as police attacked the marchers with tear gas and guns. The uprisings continued for months, spreading to Black townships across the country as the focus expanded from education to the broader injustices of the segregated nation. Hundreds of people were killed, many of them children.

At colleges across the United States—from the University of California, Berkeley, to the University of North Carolina at Chapel Hill, to Brown University in Providence, Rhode Island—students organized protests to show their support for the victims of the Soweto uprising and to push universities to pull their investments from South African companies that supported the racist apartheid regime. The young activists occupied campus buildings and built shantytowns—temporary shelters similar to those that Black South Africans in the country's slums lived in. "It was an illustration really, a constant reminder that these are the conditions of people living in South Africa, that we are, with our money, with our U.S. money, with our Brown University money, supporting the regime that allows people to live in conditions like this," Maria Testa, one of the student protesters, told *The Brown Daily Herald* in 2018.

In 1986, four students at Brown staged a hunger strike to increase the pressure on the school to divest. Although they were unsuccessful in the moment, ending their strike after ten days when it became clear that the university wasn't going to budge, their actions contributed to a wider movement that would ultimately result in the downfall of apartheid. "Within a year, Congress passed the

Students carry picket signs during a citywide boycott to protest inequality in New York's public schools on February 3, 1964. Led by local civil rights activists, the strike drew more than one-third of the city's one million students.

Students at Columbia University hold an anti-apartheid rally on April 24, 1985, after delivering a petition to the school's president calling for him to divest from companies that did business with South Africa.

comprehensive anti-Apartheid sanctions act, which had a huge impact. And then, within a number of years thereafter, Nelson Mandela was released. The country was completely transformed," Paul Zimmerman, one of the hunger strikers, recalled. "Now, did my fast do all that? Of course not. But were people like me doing their part all around the country and, frankly, all around the world? Did that contribute to international pressure? I really believe that the answer to that question is, yes, it did."

The legacy of youth-powered activism continues to this day. In 2015, students at three Philadelphia high schools walked out of their classrooms to protest proposed school budget cuts in a city where public schools are severely underfunded.

"We are not hooligans messing around," one student, Dotan Yarden, told a local news crew. "We are serious about our education, civil rights, and letting our teachers know how much we care about them."

The students were fighting for a better education not just for themselves, but also for the young people who were coming up after them. "I only have two years left," Yarden said. "I want the kids who come after me to have a better school than I had."

Three years later, in Sweden, when Greta Thunberg decided to skip school to sit outside her country's parliament and demand that lawmakers work to address climate change, she expressed a similar hope of leaving a better world for the next generation. At first the fifteen-year-old was alone. But others started to join her in FridaysForFuture—weekly school strikes that soon grew to hundreds of thousands of students all around the world taking a stand for the future of the planet. Thunberg was invited to speak at the World Economic Forum in Davos, Switzerland; at the European Parliament; and at the United Nations, where she chastised the adult leaders for failing in their responsibility to preserve the Earth for her and her peers and those who would come next. "We can't just continue living as if there was no tomorrow, because there is a tomorrow," she told *Time* in 2019, when the magazine named her Person of the Year for

The sixteen-year-old Swedish activist Greta Thunberg waits to address the crowd at a climate change protest in Manhattan's Battery Park on September 20, 2019–part of a global climate strike that drew hundreds of thousands of demonstrators around the world. "Change is coming whether they like it or not," she told the crowd, adding, "Do you think they hear us?"

At least sixty thousand people, many of them students, turned out for the New York climate strike. "I feel hopeful seeing the power of all these people here today, calling to end fossil fuels and build a better future for us," thirteen-year-old Marisol Rivera, one of the event's organizers, told *The New York Times.*

her activism. "We showed that we are united and that we, young people, are unstoppable."

Other young people have used the power of the pen—or the keyboard—to make their voices heard. In March 2016, an eight-year-old girl named Mari Copeny took a bold step to protest the poor water conditions in her hometown of Flint, Michigan. The state had changed the town's water source from the city of Detroit to the Flint River in 2014, and the new water was contaminated with lead and other chemicals, causing severe health problems among the town's residents and forcing them to rely on bottled water to drink, cook, brush their teeth, and even bathe. It was especially dangerous

for kids: lead poisoning can damage the brain and cause irreversible developmental disabilities in young people. Copeny, who called herself "Little Miss Flint," started raising money and passing out water bottles to those who needed them. When the situation dragged on unresolved, she decided to take it to the top. She wrote a letter to then-President Barack Obama, explaining to him that she was one of the many children in her community affected by the water crisis. "I've been doing my best to march in protest and to speak out for all the kids that live here in Flint," she wrote. She also offered to meet with him in Washington, where she was traveling to watch Michigan's governor testify about the situation.

"My mom said chances are you will be too busy with more important things, but there is a lot of people coming on these buses and even just a meeting from you or your wife would really lift people's spirits," she said.

The president wrote her back, applauding her activism. "You're right that Presidents are often busy, but the truth is, in America, there is no more important title than citizen," he replied. "And I am so proud of you for using your voice to speak out on behalf of the children of Flint." A few weeks later he came to Michigan to see the crisis for himself, to pledge to the people of Flint that the federal government had their back and was going to fix the crisis, and to meet Copeny. "When something like this happens, a young girl shouldn't have to go to Washington to be heard," Obama told the crowd at a local high school. "I thought her president should come to Flint to meet with her."

In 2020, the state of Michigan announced that it would pay a settlement of at least $600 million to the victims of the Flint water crisis. Nearly 80 percent of that money will go to the city's children. Copeny has continued to speak out, not just for clean water and environmental justice—raising money and donating water filters for people in Flint and other communities—but for issues like racial justice as well. In the summer of 2020, like so many young people, she took to the streets in her community, chanting that Black lives matter.

Being young, Copeny says, is no excuse for not getting involved: "There are lots of things you can do even if you can't vote. You can write letters. You can go to protests. You can post online to educate others. Anybody can make a difference. As long as we stay focused, we can make change happen. One voice is powerful. Even if you're a kid, your voice is still powerful. You have to use it."

For Thunberg, Copeny, and youth organizers like them, activism isn't an extracurricular activity. It's a calling—one that transforms rage and frustration into hope.

The activist Mari Copeny and her sister Keilani, then twelve and seven, march in a Black Lives Matter youth protest in Flint, Michigan, on June 12, 2020.

Tiana Day, a seventeen-year-old in San Ramon, California (pictured on page 130), was looking for a way to channel that rage and frustration when Black Lives Matter protests exploded across the country in the spring and early summer of 2020. "I have always had this, like, boiling thing, this boiling passion in my body to want to make a change in the world. I just never knew what it was," she told Jessica Bennett, a journalist at *The New York Times*. Day saw an Instagram comment from another teen—nineteen-year-old Mimi Zoila—who, channeling those same feelings, had gotten a permit for a protest and wanted somebody from the Black community to help lead it. (Zoila is white.) Day DMed her, and in eighteen hours the two had organized the entire thing, she said. They shared a flyer, thinking maybe fifty people would show up to march with them across the Golden Gate Bridge. In the end, there were thousands.

"We bought three cases of water because we thought it was enough. It was like four miles straight of people who were there to support the movement and honestly, most of them weren't even Black. They were allies. It was so beautiful,"

A June 4, 2020, Black Lives Matter march organized by Nashville's Teens 4 Equality—a group of girls, including Zee Thomas, all between fourteen and sixteen years old—drew around ten thousand demonstrators.

Day said. "I think I found myself through this movement."

Thousands of miles away in Nashville, Zee Thomas, fifteen, was experiencing something similar. She had never been to a protest, much less led one. But George Floyd's killing inspired her to stand up and do something. She connected with five other girls on Twitter who felt the same way; calling themselves Teens 4 Equality, they decided to organize a march for Black Lives Matter. About ten thousand people showed up. "We didn't have a podium or anything, we were standing on water coolers to speak," Thomas told Bennett. "I'm an introvert, and when I got up there I was like, 'Oh my God, what am I doing?' But I kept going."

The experience might have been scary in the moment, but ultimately, she said, it showed the power that just a few

people, even young people, have to make change possible. "As teens, we feel like we cannot make a difference in this world, but we must," she said.

Sometimes activists emerge to meet the moment. But sometimes the moment chooses them.

When a gunman walked into Marjory Stoneman Douglas High School in Parkland, Florida, with an automatic rifle on Valentine's Day 2018 and killed seventeen members of their community, the students who survived refused to let the nation forget. Traumatized, exhausted, and grieving, they immediately went to work, telling their friends' stories and demanding that the adults in power take steps to ensure that no other students ever joined the terrible club of those who had been affected by this kind of tragedy.

They created a hashtag, #neveragain, that made the nation take notice. They met with President Donald Trump and rallied lawmakers in their state capital of Tallahassee. On the one-month anniversary of the shooting, a million students from some three thousand schools participated in an Enough! National School Walkout in solidarity with the teens of Parkland, exiting their classrooms for seventeen minutes—one minute for each victim of the shooting. And on March 24, 2018, the Parkland students organized the March for Our Lives in Washington, DC: a protest to end gun violence.

"You can see very clearly in those early interviews that all of us had deep dark circles under our eyes," Emma González, then eighteen and one of the leaders of the students' movement, later wrote. But no matter how exhausted they were, they couldn't let up. "None of us wanted to stop working. To stop working was to start thinking," she said. "And thinking about anything other than the march and the solutions to gun violence was to have a breakdown."

The march drew eight hundred thousand people to the capital. Another million people attended more than eight hundred concurrent events all over the country and around the world. (In the crowd at the march in Atlanta was John Lewis, once again marching for change.) The Parkland kids invited students from across the country who had also been affected by school shootings and gun violence to join them onstage and speak about their communities. Every speaker at the march was a teenager or younger.

One of them was Yolanda Renee King, the nine-year-old granddaughter of Martin Luther King. Standing on the same ground where her grandfather had rallied a generation to fight for civil rights, she echoed his words. "I have a dream that enough is enough," she said.

The speeches were filled with grief and frustration and defiance and impatience, but also with hope for what all these people could accomplish, together.

Thousands of people flooded the streets in Washington, DC—and in more than eight hundred other cities in all fifty states—for the March for Our Lives on March 24, 2018.

Cameron Kasky, eighteen, one of the protest's organizers, thanked the thousands of marchers, many of them young people, for showing up and standing together for a better future—and for giving a nation hope.

"The march is not the climax of this movement," he said. "It is the beginning."

Three years later, Brandon Dasent, another Parkland survivor turned activist, spoke to the *New York Times* reporter John Eligon about the progress the movement had made. "We haven't done everything that we set out to do,

by any means," he said. "But in terms of getting people to listen, in terms of garnering as many eyes and ears as we possibly can, I feel like we've done that effectively."

Today, Dasent is focused on combating the scourge of police brutality by changing how officers are trained. "It shouldn't take only twenty-two weeks to graduate from a police academy when it's going to take me four years to get a film degree," he said.

Activism is, more often than not, long, slow work. It's easy in the moment to feel like one small action isn't making a difference. The scales can seem too imbalanced for one person to tip them. But protest is the work of the collective, not the individual. The power lies in the people when they join together in the fight. Each generation builds on the work of the one before and lays the foundation for the one that will follow. Progress does not happen overnight. But with perseverance, determination, and hope, the people can work to make this union a little more perfect.

"It starts with being aware of what's happening around you," seventeen-year-old Thandiwe Abdullah, a founder of the Black Lives Matter Youth Vanguard, said in an interview

Nine-year-old Yolanda Renee King, left, joins seventeen-year-old Jaclyn Corin, a survivor of the Parkland shooting and one of the March for Our Lives organizers, on stage at the rally in Washington.

for this book. "The more you pay attention to the things that are happening in your own community, the more you can start to ask questions. Why are there no trees in my neighborhood? Why are some kids' schools better than the ones in my area? Why are some people being deemed unworthy of love and care and resources just because of who they are or where they live or how they look?"

She doesn't know what the future holds, but she's optimistic about the momentum that is carrying the movement forward. "You just have to keep pushing, and keep asking questions, and keep finding people who understand why this work matters," she said. The road ahead may be long but, Abdullah says, the quest for equality and justice is worth it.

"We have to focus on freedom."

AUTHORS' NOTE

On April 20, 2021, as we were proofreading this book, the world awaited the verdict in the case that had ignited the 2020 Black Lives Matter protests. Just under a year after he knelt on George Floyd's neck, Derek Chauvin was standing trial on three charges: second-degree murder, third-degree murder, and second-degree manslaughter. There had been, from the beginning, very close attention paid to the trial and how it was being covered. People were urged to refer to the case as the Derek Chauvin murder trial as opposed to the George Floyd trial, pushing back against the problematic framing of the victim as the one on trial. President Joe Biden took the unusual step of weighing in as the sequestered jury deliberated, telling reporters that he was "praying for the right verdict."

The jury deliberated for ten hours. When the verdict came—guilty on all counts—it was seen by many as a victory in the movement for racial equity and police accountability. "This can be a giant step forward in the march toward justice in America," Biden said after it was announced.

But that movement, which seeks to undo centuries of systemic racism, extends far beyond one trial. As our colleagues John Eligon and Shawn Hubler reported three days before the verdict, "Since testimony began on March 29, at least sixty-four people have died at the hands of law enforcement nationwide, with Black and Latino people representing more than half of the dead. As of Saturday, the average was more than three killings a day." Even as the jury deliberated, protests were once again spreading around Minneapolis in response to the killing of yet another Black man by police.

There is no easy way to end this book. Sadly, the violence continues. The work of the activists, protesters, lawmakers, journalists, and concerned Americans we've profiled here is unfinished. This story is far from over. —V.C. and J.H.

IN THEIR OWN WORDS: CONVERSATIONS WITH BLACK LIVES MATTER LEADERS

These interviews have been edited for length and clarity.

ALICIA GARZA

Alicia Garza, seen speaking at a town hall in 2015, is a cofounder of Black Lives Matter and the founder of Black Futures Lab, which works to build Black political power at the local, state, and national level.

You've been an activist since middle school. What is your advice for kids who may feel nervous about stepping forward as leaders?

When we look at history, or even when we look at contemporary people who get elevated as leaders, they're not all charismatic. They're not all people who love to be in front of crowds. But they are people who care about other people. And they are people who oftentimes have been quietly helping people for years and then somebody notices what they're doing.

What would you say to people who are so afraid of doing the wrong thing that they do nothing at all?

It's totally normal. I too have that streak of perfectionism, but I realized over time that it's the mistakes that actually lead you to the breakthroughs.

And if anybody on the planet knew exactly what needed to happen at any given time and executed it perfectly, we wouldn't have to do this work.

What's your best advice about figuring out where you might make a difference?

For a lot of us, there is a thing that keeps us awake at night—a nagging feeling that things aren't right. Pay attention to what it is that moves you, like *really* moves you. For some people, it's science. For other people, it's collective action. For other people, it's writing. Whatever it is, just lean into it.

Why does protest matter?

It's one place where you can make your desires known. And it is also a place where we demonstrate that we are the majority: those of us who want to see a world that is more just and more equal.

MELINA, THANDIWE, AND AMARA ABDULLAH

Melina Abdullah with, from left, her daughter Amara; her son, Amen; and her daughter Thandiwe in 2020. Melina is a professor of Pan-African studies at California State University, Los Angeles, and a founder of Black Lives Matter Los Angeles. Thandiwe, seventeen, and Amara, fourteen, are founders of Black Lives Matter Youth Vanguard.

Melina, your whole family has been deeply involved in Black Lives Matter since the beginning. Why was that important to you?

My children have been raised in movement—Thandiwe first spoke at a protest when she was four—so just like I don't remember my first demonstration, I doubt if they do. Black Lives Matter Los Angeles was the first chapter, and we were deliberate about building it as a safe space for children. I remember one of the early meetings, my son was about three, and he was running around the space and making a lot of noise. Someone, a man, complained. And we wound up making the man leave, because we were very clear that this was a space where mothers and children and families could be. There was no expectation that children were supposed to be quiet. Children should engage in this work. And if they're running around, well, that's what three-year-olds do!

How would you define Black Lives Matter?

Black Lives Matter is a rallying cry. It is a mantra of sorts. It is a movement. And it's also a network and an organization. It's all those things. Organizations are really about how we vision and build toward the world in which we want to live. And Black Lives Matter does this all over the world. Each chapter is semiautonomous, but we're bound together by a set of guiding principles.

Amara, you and your sister have worked together to get police out of Los Angeles public schools. What made you want to take a stand?

There was a moment when I started to realize, okay, I'm one of the kids who the administration is going to call the school police on a lot. I'm one of the kids who they're going to target during random searches. And when you realize that—and you realize how other kids are also affected so much by this mentality that Black youth are never going to succeed—then you can't just sit there.

The more consistent we are with our organizing, the more progress we make. We've gotten random searches ended in schools. We got $25 million cut from the school police budget last year. That's what keeps me going.

Thandiwe, how do you deal with friends who don't understand your commitment to activism?

I've definitely lost friends throughout my entire childhood. Because I couldn't be friends with someone who didn't understand that these experiences are the top priority. If this isn't your top priority, I don't know what you're doing.

We've made a lot of progress. But where we're at now is a place where people want to believe, "Okay, now racism is over, and I don't have to do the intense labor that is necessary for freedom work." People want it to be true—especially, a lot of the times, the parents of non-Black kids. But the reality is, if you're Black, you're going to notice that you don't have freedom yet. You know racism is not over, because you live that experience.

Something Patrisse Cullors told me was that sometimes you're just going to have to leave people behind. I think she was quoting Angela Davis. Sometimes you don't need to unite with everyone. Sometimes people aren't where you need them to be. And that's okay. You've just got to let them go.

JOHNETTA ELZIE

Johnetta Elzie, pictured at an *Essence* magazine event honoring Black women in music in 2016, is a cofounder of the advocacy group Campaign Zero, which works to end police violence in the United States. She also helped found We the Protesters, which provides resources for organizers across the United States.

In your career, you've focused on working with local organizers. Why is that important to you?

I am trying to fill in the blanks and fill in the gaps that I wish someone had actually made a real effort to do when they came to Ferguson seven years ago. The people already live there; they're doing their work. We're just here to support. If you need to meet with legislators to get a bill on the board? Let's do that. You need graphics? Here's the team. You need experts to prove that the data we're presenting to you is accurate, or your stakeholders need to talk to actual experts? We've got that.

What advice do you have for young people who want to get involved but don't know how?

I would say, ask your friends, because they probably want to get involved and also don't know how. And then, boom, suddenly you can come together and come up with ideas. Then from there, boom, make another plan. How do we do what we want to do?

That's what we did in 2014. I didn't go out with some activist group. I went with my best friend, who has been my friend since I was fourteen years old. Then the next day I went with her and her cousin and another best friend. So it just kept growing.

Generally, your friends are like-minded people. So chances are, if you care, they care.

DERAY MCKESSON

DeRay Mckesson is an activist, educator, and cofounder of Campaign Zero. He is pictured working on the *Ferguson Protester Newsletter*, which he cofounded with Elzie and others, in 2014.

Campaign Zero is dedicated to reforming the way policing in America works. Can you explain what you mean by that?

No matter what happens today in America, there will likely be police officers tomorrow. Campaign Zero believes they should have less power tomorrow. We think that's not a dramatic idea.

When you're dealing with so much tragedy and death in your work, how do you keep from being overwhelmed?

The thing I always say is that one is the biggest number. One is your mother. One is your sister. One is your brother. One is a huge number. And if we can help get to one less death, that's a good thing.

How did your years in student government prepare you for what you do now?

I was in student government from sixth grade until my senior year in college. At Bowdoin College, I was the first person to ever be class president and student body president at the same time. And what I learned was that people want to be in community, no matter what they say. That's why they go to homecoming. That's why they get into Spirit Week and sports games. They will be stubborn about it or act like they're too cool, but they want to be in community.

And I also learned that community doesn't just emerge. You have to build it.

As a protester, you've faced tear gas, arrests, and many other things that must have been scary. How do you get past the fear?

I had to realize that fear is human. The question becomes: How do you make sure that fear is not the only emotion or the biggest emotion present? So in moments when I get nervous or sad, I'm like, DeRay, you ain't got forever. And I want to know that I did my part while I had a chance to do my part.

RESOURCES

FURTHER READING

Dear Martin by Nic Stone (Crown Books, 2017)

Freedom Walkers: The Story of the Montgomery Bus Boycott by Russell Freedman (Holiday House, 2006)

Ghost Boys by Jewell Parker Rhodes (Little, Brown, 2018)

Harbor Me by Jacqueline Woodson (Nancy Paulsen Books, 2018)

The Hate U Give by Angie Thomas (Balzer + Bray, 2017)

It's Trevor Noah: Born a Crime; Stories from a South African Childhood (Adapted for Young Readers) by Trevor Noah (Delacorte Press, 2019)

Just Mercy: A True Story of the Fight for Justice (Adapted for Young Adults) by Bryan Stevenson (Delacorte Press, 2018)

March (Books One, Two, and Three) by John Lewis and Andrew Aydin, illustrated by Nate Powell (Top Shelf Productions, 2016)

March Forward, Girl: From Young Warrior to Little Rock Nine by Melba Pattillo Beals, illustrated by Frank Morrison (Houghton Mifflin Harcourt, 2018)

Not My Idea: A Book About Whiteness by Anastasia Higginbotham (Dottir Press, 2018)

Punching the Air by Ibi Zoboi and Yusef Salaam, illustrated by Omar T. Pasha (Balzer + Bray, 2020)

Resist: 40 Profiles of Ordinary People Who Rose Up Against Tyranny and Injustice by Veronica Chambers, illustrated by Paul Ryding (HarperCollins, 2020)

Stamped: Racism, Antiracism, and You (A Remix of the National Book Award–winning *Stamped from the Beginning*) by Jason Reynolds and Ibram X. Kendi (Little, Brown, 2020)

The Stars Beneath Our Feet by David Barclay Moore (Alfred A. Knopf, 2017)

This Book Is Anti-Racist: 20 Lessons on How to Wake Up, Take Action, and Do the Work by Tiffany Jewell, illustrated by Aurélia Durand (Frances Lincoln, 2020)

Together We March: 25 Protest Movements That Marched into History by Leah Henderson, illustrated by Tyler Feder (Atheneum Books, 2021)

Turning 15 on the Road to Freedom: My Story of the 1965 Selma Voting Rights March by Lynda Blackmon Lowery as told to Elspeth Leacock and Susan Buckley, illustrated by PJ Loughran (Dial Books, 2015)

We Are Power: How Nonviolent Activism Changes the World by Todd Hasak-Lowy (Abrams Books, 2020)

We Rise, We Resist, We Raise Our Voices, edited by Wade Hudson and Cheryl Willis Hudson (Crown Books, 2018)

We Shall Overcome: A Song That Changed the World by Stuart Stotts, illustrated by Terrance Cummings (Clarion Books, 2010)

When They Call You a Terrorist: A Story of Black Lives Matter and the Power to Change the World (Young Adult Edition) by Patrisse Khan-Cullors and asha bandele, adapted with Benee Knauer (Wednesday Books, 2020)

Woke: A Young Poet's Call to Justice by Mahogany L. Browne with Elizabeth Acevedo and Olivia Gatwood, illustrated by Theodore Taylor III (Roaring Brook Press, 2020)

ACKNOWLEDGMENTS

If you've ever had the pleasure of hearing Kwame Alexander read from one of his incredible books, you know that the griot tradition is alive and well. So when Kwame and Margaret Raymo called us about this project, the only sensible response was yes. We're honored that this is our second book with Versify, and we're grateful to our editors at The New York Times—Caroline Que and Monica Drake—who made working on this book possible.

This book is built upon the work of the incredible photographers and photo editors who have covered this story for years. Thank you to our photo editor, Anika Burgess, for being so good at what you do and for approaching this topic with both expertise and sensitivity.

We couldn't have made this book without the work of New York Times editors Brian Gallagher and Nick Donofrio. The Past Tense team—Veronica, Jennifer, Brian, Nick, and Anika—will always be a journalism super band. (And we mean you, too, Jessie Wender.)

Our deepest thanks to the Versify team, especially our editor, Weslie Turner; art director, Whitney Leader-Picone; associate art director, Samira Iravani; and designer, Monique Sterling. We're so happy to have gotten a chance to tap the creativity of Mary Claire Cruz. Thanks as well to the extended HMH team, including Mary Magrisso, Erika West, Maxine Bartow, Susan Bishansky, Lisa DiSarro, Julie Yeater, Tara Shanahan, and Taylor McBroom.

We are lucky to know and work with Ellen Archer as well as the Inkwell Management team, Kimberly Witherspoon and Jessica Mileo.

At The New York Times, we're grateful for the editing and reporting expertise of Jamie Stockwell, Dodai Stewart, and John Eligon. The Special Projects team kept us fueled with their creativity and support. Thank you (again) to Monica Drake for being such an inspiring leader, and to our colleagues Heather Phillips, Lauren Messman, Adam Sternbergh, David Klopfenstein, and Jeremy Allen for all your help.

The Metro team let us use their insightful story "From Bike Blockers to Street Medics: The Anatomy of an N.Y.C. Protest" in the book. For that, we thank Juliana Kim, Simbarashe Cha, Lily Benson, Meghan Louttit, Andrew Hinderaker, and Clifford Levy.

From the moment we knew that the pictures would lead in this book, the Times photo and design teams helped us shape and imagine what it could be. Thank you to photo editors Meaghan Looram, Nakyung Han, Beth Flynn, Becky Lebowitz, and Crista Chapman for your unmatched insight and keen eyes, and to Kelly Doe, Jason Fujikuni, and Carrie Mifsud for your time and creativity.

We could not have made this book without the help of the art production team, in particular Steve Brown, David Braun, and Sonny Figueroa. And William O'Donnell is more than an editor: he is a fount of wisdom about the incredible people who were staff photographers for The Times throughout the twentieth century. It's because of him that we know and love the work of Don Hogan Charles, Chester Higgins Jr., George Tames, Sam Falk, and so many others. Thank you, Bill, for being so generous with us.

Sarah Borell helped us with the many (many, many) clearances. The legal team at The Times—especially Simone Procas, Lee Riffaterre, and Irina Starkova—took all our calls, as did Alexander Smith in licensing. Rogene Jacquette helped us navigate important questions of standards. And Ari Isaacman Bevacqua and Annie Tressler made sure our work got out into the world.

It's always a little scary the first time you send a draft to outside readers. Thank you to Kawan Allen, Somini Sengupta, Lynette Clemetson, Ellis Clemetson, Jason Clampet, and Flora Clampet for your detailed notes and feedback. And a huge thanks as well to Laura Bullard and Anakwa Dwamena for making sure we got all the facts right.

Caroline Que not only leads the incredible enterprise that is New York Times Book Development, but she is also one of the best line editors in town. Thank you, Caroline, for making every page of this book stronger and for keeping us going with your encouragement and support.

Finally, we'd like to thank the scholars and leaders who took the time to talk to us for this book: the Reverend Leah Daughtry, Professor Thomas J. Sugrue, Johnetta Elzie, DeRay Mckesson, Melina Abdullah, Thandiwe Abdullah, and Amara Abdullah. And a special thank you to Alicia Garza for drawing us a map with your words, from that first Facebook post to the Black Futures Lab —V.C. and J.H.

PHOTO CREDITS

Back Cover (clockwise from top right)—Michael A. McCoy for The New York Times, Demetrius Freeman for The New York Times, Gabriela Bhaskar for The New York Times, Simbarashe Cha for The New York Times, Simbarashe Cha for The New York Times, Paul Christian Gordon/Alamy

Table of Contents—Demetrius Freeman for The New York Times (p. vi)

Introduction: A Transformative Summer—Simbarashe Cha for The New York Times (p. viii), Victor J. Blue for The New York Times (p. 2), Alyssa Schukar for The New York Times (p. 2), Michael A. McCoy for The New York Times (p. 2), Demetrius Freeman for The New York Times (p. 3), Brandon Bell for The New York Times (p. 3), Sylvain Cherkaoui/AP/Shutterstock (p. 4), Laylah Amatullah Barrayn for The New York Times (p. 5)

In Pictures: This Is What Protest Looks Like—Amir Hamja for The New York Times (p. 7), Whitney Curtis for The New York Times (p. 8), Xavier Burrell for The New York Times (p. 9), Demetrius Freeman for The New York Times (p. 10), Simbarashe Cha for The New York Times (p. 11), Kayla Reefer for The New York Times (p. 11), Demetrius Freeman for The New York Times (pp. 12–13), Amir Hamja for The New York Times (p. 14), Erin Schaff/The New York Times (pp. 14–15), Demetrius Freeman for The New York Times (p. 15)

Chapter 1: Three Girls Who Wanted to Make the World Better—Kevork Djansezian/Getty Images for Glamour (p. 16), ZUMA Press/Alamy (p. 18), Jamie McCarthy/Getty Images (p. 19), Paul Morigi/Getty Images (p. 21), Gabriela Bhaskar for The New York Times (p. 23)

Chapter 2: It Started With A Love Letter—Demetrius Freeman for The New York Times (p. 24), Damon Winter/The New York Times (p. 27), AP Images (p. 28), Demetrius Freeman for The New York Times (p. 29)

Chapter 3: A Moment Becomes a Movement—Whitney Curtis for The New York Times (p. 30), Wally Skalij/Los Angeles Times via Getty Images (p. 32), Whitney Curtis for The New York Times (p. 33), Whitney Curtis for The New York Times (p. 34), Paras Griffin/Getty Images (p. 35), Allyn Baum/The New York Times (p. 37), Courtesy of the Archives and Records Services Division, Mississippi Department of Archives and History (p. 39), Matt McClain/The Washington Post via Getty Images (p. 43)

Chapter 4: So Many Ways to Be an Activist—Zach Gibson for The New York Times (p. 44), Arthur Schatz/The LIFE Picture Collection via Getty Images (p. 47), Todd Heisler/The New York Times (p. 48), Joshua Lott for The New York Times (p. 49), Whitney Curtis for The New York Times (p. 50), Jacquelyn Martin/AP/Shutterstock (p. 52)

Timelines: A Change Is Gonna Come—The New York Times (p. 54), George Tames/The New York Times (p. 55), George Tames/The New York Times (p. 56), Rowland Scherman/National Archives (542030) (p.57), Neal Boenzi/The New York Times (p. 59), Michael Appleton for The New York Times (p. 60), Michelle V. Agins/The New York Times (p. 62), Gabriella Demczuk for The New York Times (p. 63), Erin Schaff/The New York Times (p. 65)

Chapter 5: What Is Systemic Racism?—Photograph by Gordon Parks. Courtesy of and copyright The Gordon Parks Foundation (p. 66); Don Hogan Charles/The New York Times (p. 68); John Vachon, via Library of Congress Prints and Photographs Division (p. 71); Johnson Publishing Company Archive. Courtesy of Ford Foundation, J. Paul Getty Trust, John D. and Catherine T. MacArthur Foundation, Andrew W. Mellon Foundation, and Smithsonian Institution (p. 72); Howard Sochurek/The LIFE Picture Collection via Getty Images (p. 73); Bettmann/Getty Images (p. 74); Eddie Hausner/The New York Times (p. 75)

Chapter 6: How Champions Lead—Ezra Shaw/Getty Images (p. 76), Michelle V. Agins/The New York Times (p. 80), Larry C. Morris/The New York Times (p. 82), AP Images (p. 83), The Asahi Shimbun via Getty Images (p. 84), Mike Lien/The New York Times (p. 85), Jason Szenes/EPA-EFE via Shutterstock (p. 86), Matthew Stockman/Getty Images (p. 86), Al Bello/Getty Images (p. 86), Matthew Stockman/Getty Images (pp. 86–87), Matthew Stockman/Getty Images (p. 87), Matthew Stockman/Getty Images (p. 87), Al Bello/Getty Images (p. 87)

Chapter 7: Lift Every Voice and Sing—Simbarashe Cha for The New York Times (p. 88), William Gottlieb/Redferns via Getty Images (p. 91), National Archives (542025) (p. 93), Leon Bennett/WireImage via Getty Images (p. 94), Albin Lohr-Jones/Pacific Press/LightRocket via Getty Images (p. 95, top), Hiroko Masuike/The New York Times (p. 95, bottom)

Visual Moment: Murals With a Message—Carlos Vilas Delgado/EPA via Shutterstock (p. 99); Photo: Elijah Nouvelage/Getty Images, Mural: The Loss Prevention Arts (p. 100); Photo: Laylah Amatullah Barrayn for The New York Times, Mural: Menace Two and Resa Piece @menaceresa (p. 101); Photo: Joshua Lott for The Washington Post/Getty Images, Mural: Braylyn "Resko" Stewart, Whitney Holbourn, and Andrew Norris (p. 102); Photo: Joshua Rashaad McFadden for The New York Times, Mural: Cadex Herrera, Greta McLain, and Xena Goldman (p. 103); Photo: Travis Young, Mural: Rodney "Lucky" Easterwood and Anita Easterwood, @luckyeasterwoodart and @anita_easterwood (p. 104); Photo: Ryan C. Hermens, Mural: Ciara LeRoy @prettystrangedesign (pp. 104–105); Photo: Images-USA/Alamy, Mural: Camila Ibarra (p. 105); Photo: John Christie, Mural, lead artists: L. C. Howard, Gina Martinez, John Christie, and Joy Johnson (pp. 106–107); Sarahbeth Maney (p. 107)

Chapter 8: The Art of Protest—Victor J. Blue for The New York Times (p. 108); Carl T. Gossett Jr./The New York Times (p. 110); Collection of the Smithsonian National Museum of African American History and Culture, Gift of Samuel Y. Edgerton (p. 110); Demetrius Freeman for The New York Times (p. 111); Sean Rayford for The New York Times (p. 112); Courtesy of Nikkolas Smith (p. 114); Photo: Sue Kwon. Courtesy of Jammie Holmes and Library Street Collective (p. 115)

A Closer Look: Who's Who at a Protest—Simbarashe Cha for The New York Times (p. 117), Simbarashe Cha for The New York Times (p. 117), Hiroko Masuike/The New York Times (p. 118, top), Michael Noble Jr. for The New York Times (p. 118, bottom), Simbarashe Cha for The New York Times (p. 119), Simbarashe Cha for The New York Times (p. 119)

Chapter 9: What People Power Can Do—Joshua Rashaad McFadden for The New York Times (p. 120), Chloe Collyer for The New York Times (p. 122), Michael A. McCoy for The New York Times (p. 124), Gabriela Bhaskar for The New York Times (p. 125), Demetrius Freeman for The New York Times (p. 127), Whitney Curtis for The New York Times (p. 128)

Chapter 10: Never Too Young to Lead—John G. Mabanglo/EPA-EFE/Shutterstock (p. 130), Bettmann/Getty Images (p. 132), Eddie Hausner/The New York Times (p. 133), Chester Higgins Jr./The New York Times (p. 134), Damon Winter/The New York Times (p. 135), Damon Winter/The New York Times (p. 135), Jake May/MLive.com/The Flint Journal via AP (p. 136), Alex Kent/Shutterstock (p. 137), Erin Schaff for The New York Times (p. 139), Paul Morigi/Getty Images for March For Our Lives (p. 140)

In Their Own Words: Conversations With Black Lives Matter Leaders—Earl Gibson III/Getty Images (p. 142), Valerie Macon/AFP via Getty Images (p. 142), Jason LaVeris/FilmMagic via Getty Images (p. 143), Sid Hastings for The Washington Post via Getty Images (p. 144)

SELECTED BIBLIOGRAPHY

In writing this book, we had the unusual experience of researching history as it was occurring. We relied heavily on conversations with and reporting by our New York Times colleagues who were on the ground covering the 2020 protests, many of whom had been writing about Black Lives Matter and the struggle for racial justice for years. Much of their work is included in the list below. We also spoke with many leaders of the Black Lives Matter movement, from those who had been there since the beginning to activists moved by the events of 2020. Their recollections and insights were invaluable as we put together this book.

This is a partial list of our sources, which we hope will be useful to parents, teachers, and librarians. We relied on numerous web pages maintained by the National Archives; the Library of Congress; the National Park Service; the National Museum of African American History and Culture; the Martin Luther King, Jr. Research and Education Institute at Stanford University; the University System of Georgia's Civil Rights Digital Library; the SNCC Digital Gateway; and the University of North Carolina at Chapel Hill's Documenting the American South project. URLs accompany sources that were freely available online at the time of writing. Britannica Academic was a general reference.

Abdullah, Thandiwe. "I March for Black Girls and the Black Women Who Marched Before Me." *Refinery29*, Oct. 10, 2019. www.refinery29.com/en-us/2019/10/8541898/thandiwe-abdullah-black-lives-matter-youth-vanguard.

Alvarez, Lizette. "Florida Sit-In Against 'Stand Your Ground.'" *New York Times*, Aug. 11, 2013. www.nytimes.com/2013/08/12/us/dream-defenders-arent-walking-out-on-their-florida-protest.html.

Amoako, Aida. "Strange Fruit: The Most Shocking Song of All Time?" *BBC*, Apr. 17, 2019. www.bbc.com/culture/article/20190415-strange-fruit-the-most-shocking-song-of-all-time.

Anderson, Melinda D. "Why Are So Many Preschoolers Getting Suspended?" *Atlantic*, Dec. 7, 2015. www.theatlantic.com/education/archive/2015/12/why-are-so-many-preschoolers-getting-suspended/418932.

Anderson, Monica, and Paul Hitlin. "Social Media Conversations about Race." Pew Research Center. Aug. 15, 2016. www.pewresearch.org/internet/2016/08/15/social-media-conversations-about-race.

Anderson, Monica, Skye Toor, Lee Rainie, and Aaron Smith. "Activism in the Social Media Age." Pew Research Center. July 11, 2018. www.pewresearch.org/internet/2018/07/11/activism-in-the-social-media-age.

Arsenault, Raymond. "Arthur Ashe's Real Legacy Was His Activism, Not His Tennis." *Guardian*, Sept. 9, 2018. www.theguardian.com/sport/2018/sep/09/arthur-ashe-legacy-activism-tennis.

Beckert, Sven, and Seth Rockman, eds. *Slavery's Capitalism: A New History of American Economic Development*. Philadelphia: University of Pennsylvania Press, 2016.

Bennett, Jessica. "These Teen Girls Are Fighting for a More Just Future." *New York Times*, June 26, 2020. www.nytimes.com/2020/06/26/style/teen-girls-black-lives-matter-activism.html.

Bergeron, Elena. "How Putting on a Mask Raised Naomi Osaka's Voice." *New York Times*, Dec. 16, 2020. www.nytimes.com/2020/12/16/sports/tennis/naomi-osaka-protests-open.html.

Berman, Mark, John Sullivan, Julie Tate, and Jennifer Jenkins. "Protests Spread over Police Shootings. Police Promised Reforms. Every Year, They Still Shoot and Kill Nearly 1,000 People." *Washington Post*, June 8, 2020. www.washingtonpost.com/investigations/protests-spread-over-police-shootings-police-promised-reforms-every-year-they-still-shoot-nearly-1000-people/2020/06/08/5c204f0c-a67c-11ea-b473-04905b1af82b_story.html.

Boren, Cindy. "Roger Goodell Wishes the NFL 'Had Listened Earlier' to Colin Kaepernick, Supports Players Who Kneel." *Washington Post*, Aug. 24, 2020. www.washingtonpost.com/sports/2020/08/24/roger-goodell-wishes-nfl-had-listened-earlier-colin-kaepernick.

Bosman, Julie, and Emma G. Fitzsimmons. "Grief and Protests Follow Shooting of a Teenager." *New York Times*, Aug. 10, 2014. www.nytimes.com/2014/08/11/us/police-say-mike-brown-was-killed-after-struggle-for-gun.html.

Branch, John. "The Awakening of Colin Kaepernick." *New York Times*, Sept. 7, 2017. www.nytimes.com/2017/09/07/sports/colin-kaepernick-nfl-protests.html.

Brazile, Donna, Yolanda Caraway, Leah Daughtry, and Minyon Moore with Veronica Chambers. *For Colored Girls Who Have Considered Politics*. New York: St. Martin's Press, 2018.

Brown, DeNeen L. "'A Cry for Freedom': The Black Power Salute That Rocked the World 50 Years Ago."
Washington Post, Oct. 16, 2018. www.washingtonpost.com/history/2018/10/16/a-cry-freedom-black-power-salute-that-rocked-world-years-ago.

Buchanan, Jean, Adam Goodman, Matt Franck, Lynden Steele, Gary Hairlson, and Beth O'Malley. "Ferguson: As It Unfolded." *St. Louis Post-Dispatch*, Feb. 3, 2015. graphics.stltoday.com/ferguson.

Buchanan, Larry, Quoctrung Bui, and Jugal K. Patel. "Black Lives Matter May Be the Largest Movement in U.S. History." *New York Times*, July 3, 2020. www.nytimes.com/interactive/2020/07/03/us/george-floyd-protests-crowd-size.html.

Bump, Philip. "Over the Past 60 Years, More Spending on Police Hasn't Necessarily Meant Less Crime." *Washington Post*, June 7, 2020. www.washingtonpost.com/politics/2020/06/07/over-past-60-years-more-spending-police-hasnt-necessarily-meant-less-crime.

Byck, Daniella. "DC Pastry Chefs Launch a National Bake Sale to Support Black Lives Matter." *Washingtonian*, June 5, 2020. www.washingtonian.com/2020/06/05/dc-pastry-chefs-launch-a-national-bake-sale-to-support-black-lives-matter.

Calamur, Krishnadev. "When Muhammad Ali Refused to Go to Vietnam." *Atlantic*, June 4, 2016. www.theatlantic.com/news/archive/2016/06/muhammad-ali-vietnam/485717.

Carroll, Rebecca. "Brittany Packnett Cunningham on Activism in Crisis." *Come Through with Rebecca Carroll*, WNYC, Apr. 14, 2020. Audio, 35:47. www.wnycstudios.org/podcasts/come-through/articles/brittany-packnett-cunningham.

Chayka, Kyle. "The Mimetic Power of D.C.'s Black Lives Matter Mural." *New Yorker*, June 9, 2020. www.newyorker.com/culture/dept-of-design/the-mimetic-power-of-dcs-black-lives-matter-mural.

Civil Rights Digital Library. University System of Georgia. crdl.usg.edu.

Closson, Troy, and Sean Piccoli. "Thousands Join N.Y.C. Bike Protests: 'It's Like Riding in the Cavalry.'" *New York Times*, July 2, 2020. www.nytimes.com/2020/07/02/nyregion/Floyd-bike-protests-new-york.html.

Coates, Ta-Nehisi. "The Case for Reparations." *Atlantic*, June 2014. www.theatlantic.com/magazine/archive/2014/06/the-case-for-reparations/361631.

Cobb, Jelani. "The Matter of Black Lives." *New Yorker*, Mar. 7, 2016. www.newyorker.com/magazine/2016/03/14/where-is-black-lives-matter-headed.

Costello, Darcy, and Tessa Duvall. "911 Call from Breonna Taylor Shooting: 'Somebody Kicked in the Door and Shot My Girlfriend.'" *Courier-Journal*, May 28, 2020.

www.courier-journal.com/story/news/local/2020/05/28/breonna-taylor-shooting-911-call-details-aftermath-police-raid/5277489002.

Cullors, Patrisse. "'Black Lives Matter' Is About More than the Police." American Civil Liberties Union. June 23, 2020. www.aclu.org/news/criminal-law-reform/black-lives-matter-is-about-more-than-the-police.

Daniels, Gilda R. *Uncounted: The Crisis of Voter Suppression in the United States*. New York: New York University Press, 2020.

Day, Elizabeth. "#BlackLivesMatter: The Birth of a New Civil Rights Movement." *Guardian*, July 19, 2015. www.theguardian.com/world/2015/jul/19/blacklivesmatter-birth-civil-rights-movement.

Del Barco, Mandalit. "'Artivist' Nikkolas Smith Combines Art and Activism into A Singular Superpower." *NPR*, June 29, 2020. www.npr.org/2020/06/29/883490848/artivist-nikkolas-smith-combines-art-and-activism-into-a-singular-superpower.

Documenting the American South. The University Library of the University of North Carolina at Chapel Hill. docsouth.unc.edu.

Elbow, Steven. "Activists Want to 'Defund.' How Do Other Countries Curb Police Excesses?" *Capital Times*, June 27, 2020. madison.com/news/local/govt-and-politics/activists-want-to-defund-how-do-other-countries-curb-police-excesses/article_363c1712-f8e7-52ce-85cf-394e786e35a1.html.

Eligon, John. "Black Lives Matter Grows as Movement While Facing New Challenges." *New York Times*, Aug. 28, 2020. www.nytimes.com/2020/08/28/us/black-lives-matter-protest.html.

———. "The Race Beat: Straddling America's Great Divide." Apr. 25, 2017. Smith-Buonanno Hall, Brown University, Providence, RI. Video, 55:29. www.brown.edu/academics/english/events/john-eligon-talk.

———. "They Push. They Protest. And Many Activists, Privately, Suffer as a Result." *New York Times*, Mar. 26, 2018. www.nytimes.com/2018/03/26/us/they-push-they-protest-and-many-activists-privately-suffer-as-a-result.html.

Fausset, Richard. "What We Know about the Shooting Death of Ahmaud Arbery." *New York Times*, Dec. 17, 2020. www.nytimes.com/article/ahmaud-arbery-shooting-georgia.html.

Garza, Alicia. President's Lecture. Feb. 2, 2016. Ted Constant Convocation Center, Old Dominion University, Norfolk, VA. Video, 1:16:10. digitalcommons.odu.edu/pls/6.

———. *The Purpose of Power: How We Come Together When We Fall Apart*. New York: One World, 2020.

Goff, Phillip Atiba, Matthew Christian Jackson, Brooke Allison Lewis Di Leone, Carmen Marie Culotta, and Natalie Ann DiTomasso. "The Essence of Innocence: Consequences of Dehumanizing Black Children." *Journal of Personality and Social Psychology* 106, no. 4 (2014): 526–45. www.apa.org/pubs/journals/releases/psp-a0035663.pdf.

González, Emma. "A Young Activist's Advice: Vote, Shave Your Head and Cry Whenever You Need To." *New York Times*, Oct. 5, 2018. www.nytimes.com/2018/10/05/opinion/sunday/emma-gonzalez-parkland.html.

Grant, Laurens, dir. *Stay Woke: The Black Lives Matter Movement*. 2016; BET.

Greenhouse, Steven. "The Pandemic Has Intensified Systemic Economic Racism against Black Americans." *New Yorker*, July 30, 2020. www.newyorker.com/news/news-desk/the-pandemic-has-intensified-systemic-economic-racism-against-black-americans.

Griffith, Mark Winston. "Black Love Matters." *Nation*, July 2015. www.thenation.com/article/archive/black-love-matters.

Hannah-Jones, Nikole, et al. The 1619 Project. *New York Times*, Aug. 14, 2019. www.nytimes.com/interactive/2019/08/14/magazine/1619-america-slavery.html.

Heyward, Giulia L. "The Righteous Power of the George Floyd Mural." *New Republic*, June 15, 2020. newrepublic.com/article/158176/righteous-power-george-floyd-mural.

Hogan, Marc. "Black Lives Matter's DeRay Mckesson on the Power of Protest Music." *Pitchfork*, Oct. 13, 2016. pitchfork.com/thepitch/1318-black-lives-matters-deray-mckesson-on-the-power-of-protest-music.

Horowitz, Juliana Menasce, and Gretchen Livingston. "How Americans View the Black Lives Matter Movement." Pew Research Center. July 8, 2016. www.pewresearch.org/fact-tank/2016/07/08/how-americans-view-the-black-lives-matter-movement.

Jamieson, Rachel, and Patrick Johnston. "Crowd Gathers to 'Walk for Justice.'" *Havre Daily News*, June 2, 2020. www.havredailynews.com/story/2020/06/01/local/crowd-gathers-to-walk-for-justice/529125.html.

Jones, Ellen E. "Opal Tometi, Co-Founder of Black Lives Matter: 'I Do This Because We Deserve to Live.'" *Guardian*, Sept. 24, 2020. www.theguardian.com/society/2020/sep/24/opal-tometi-co-founder-of-black-lives-matter-i-do-this-because-we-deserve-to-live.

Kang, Jay Caspian. "'Our Demand Is Simple: Stop Killing Us.'" *New York Times*, May 4, 2015. www.nytimes.com/2015/05/10/magazine/our-demand-is-simple-stop-killing-us.html.

Khan-Cullors, Patrisse, and asha bandele. *When They Call You a Terrorist: A Black Lives Matter Memoir*. New York: St. Martin's Press, 2018.

Kim, Juliana, and Simbarashe Cha. "From Bike Blockers to Street Medics: The Anatomy of an N.Y.C. Protest." *New York Times*, Sept. 19, 2020. www.nytimes.com/2020/09/19/nyregion/street-protest-nyc.html.

King, Jamilah. "The Women behind #blacklivesmatter." *California Sunday Magazine*, Mar. 1, 2015. stories.californiasunday.com/2015-03-01/black-lives-matter.

Lepore, Jill. "The Invention of the Police." *New Yorker*, July 13, 2020. www.newyorker.com/magazine/2020/07/20/the-invention-of-the-police.

Lewis, John. "45 Years Since Selma, Rep. John Lewis Reflects." Interview by Neal Conan. *Talk of the Nation*, *NPR*, Mar. 8, 2010. Audio, 17:08. www.npr.org/templates/story/story.php?storyId=124461875.

Library of Congress. www.loc.gov.

Limbong, Andrew. "Both Party and Protest, 'Alright' Is the Sound of Black Life's Duality." *NPR*, Aug. 26, 2019. www.npr.org/2019/08/26/753511135/kendrick-lamar-alright-american-anthem-party-protest.

López, Carlos Andres. "Dolores Huerta: 'We Have to Keep on Marching.'" *New York Times*, Oct. 7, 2020. www.nytimes.com/2020/10/07/opinion/international-world/dolores-huerta-activists-unions.html.

Lowery, Wesley. *They Can't Kill Us All: Ferguson, Baltimore, and a New Era in America's Racial Justice Movement*. New York: Little, Brown and Company, 2016.

Lynskey, Dorian. *33 Revolutions Per Minute: A History of Protest Songs, from Billie Holiday to Green Day*. New York: Ecco, 2011.

Maese, Rick. "Two Sprinters Gave the Black-Power Salute at the Olympics. It Took Them Decades to Recover from That Gesture." *Washington Post*, May 28, 2018. www.washingtonpost.com/national/two-sprinters-gave-the-black-power-salute-at-the-olympics-it-took-them-decades-to-recover-from-that-gesture/2018/05/28/b29e9dfc-4a58-11e8-827e-190efaf1f1ee_story.html.

The Martin Luther King, Jr. Research and Education Institute. Stanford University. kinginstitute.stanford.edu.

Mckesson, DeRay. *On the Other Side of Freedom: The Case for Hope*. New York: Penguin Books, 2019.

Morales, Christina, and Kurt Streeter. "Maya Moore, W.N.B.A. Star, Marries Man She Helped Free from Prison." *New York Times*, Sept. 16, 2020. www.nytimes.com/2020/09/16/sports/basketball/maya-moore-jonathan-irons.html.

Moskin, Julia. "When the Bake Sale Goes Global, Millions Are Raised to Fight Injustice." *New York Times*, July 21, 2020. www.nytimes.com/2020/07/21/dining/bake-sale-activism-racism.html.

Moss, Hilary. "George Floyd's Final Words, Written in the Sky." *New York Times*, June 1, 2020. www.nytimes.com/2020/06/01/t-magazine/george-floyd-jammie-holmes-artist.html.

Nagourney, Adam. "Prayer, Anger and Protests Greet Verdict in Florida Case." *New York Times*, July 14, 2013. www.nytimes.com/2013/07/15/us/debate-on-race-and-justice-is-renewed.html.

National Archives. www.archives.gov.

National Museum of African American History and Culture. nmaahc.si.edu.

National Park Service. www.nps.gov.

Nodjimbadem, Katie. "The Long, Painful History of Police

Brutality in the U.S." *Smithsonian Magazine*, July 27, 2017. www.smithsonianmag.com/smithsonian-institution/long-painful-history-police-brutality-in-the-us-180964098.

Norris, Michele. "At 1963 March, a Face in the Crowd Became a Poster Child." *NPR*, Aug. 21, 2013. www.npr.org/2013/08/21/213804335/at-1963-march-a-face-in-the-crowd-became-a-poster-child.

Oppel Jr., Richard A., Derrick Bryson Taylor, and Nicholas Bogel-Burroughs. "What to Know about Breonna Taylor's Death." *New York Times*, Jan. 6, 2021. www.nytimes.com/article/breonna-taylor-police.html.

Packnett, Brittany. "Black Lives Matter Isn't Just a Hashtag Anymore." *Politico Magazine*, September/October 2016. www.politico.com/magazine/story/2016/09/black-lives-matter-movement-deray-hacknett-politics-protest-214226.

Patil, Anushka. "How a March for Black Trans Lives Became a Huge Event." *New York Times*, June 15, 2020. www.nytimes.com/2020/06/15/nyregion/brooklyn-black-trans-parade.html.

Petersen, Anne Helen. "Why the Small Protests in Small Towns across America Matter." *BuzzFeed News*, June 3, 2020. www.buzzfeednews.com/article/annehelenpetersen/black-lives-matter-protests-near-me-small-towns.

Rahim, Zamira, and Rob Picheta. "Thousands around the World Protest George Floyd's Death in Global Display of Solidarity." *CNN*, June 1, 2020. www.cnn.com/2020/06/01/world/george-floyd-global-protests-intl/index.html.

Rainey, James, Dakota Smith, and Cindy Chang. "Growing the LAPD Was Gospel at City Hall. George Floyd Changed That." *Los Angeles Times*, June 5, 2020. www.latimes.com/california/story/2020-06-05/eric-garcetti-lapd-budget-cuts-10000-officers-protests.

Randle, Aaron. "Now You See Me: A Look at the World of Activist Johnetta Elzie." *Complex*, Mar. 8, 2016. www.complex.com/life/2016/03/johnetta-elzie-profile.

Ransby, Barbara. *Making All Black Lives Matter: Reimagining Freedom in the Twenty-First Century*. Oakland: University of California Press, 2018.

Reid, Eric. "Eric Reid: Why Colin Kaepernick and I Decided to Take a Knee." *New York Times*, Sept. 25, 2017. www.nytimes.com/2017/09/25/opinion/colin-kaepernick-football-protests.html.

Robles, Frances. "A Look at What Happened the Night Trayvon Martin Died." *Miami Herald*, March 31, 2012.

Rothstein, Richard. *The Color of Law: A Forgotten History of How Our Government Segregated America*. New York: Liveright, 2017.

Rovner, Joshua. "Racial Disparities in Youth Commitments and Arrests." The Sentencing Project. Apr. 1, 2016. www.sentencingproject.org/publications/racial-disparities-in-youth-commitments-and-arrests.

Russonello, Giovanni. "Why Most Americans Support the Protests." *New York Times*, June 5, 2020. www.nytimes.

com/2020/06/05/us/politics/polling-george-floyd-protests-racism.html.

Schermerhorn, Calvin. "Why the Racial Wealth Gap Persists, More than 150 Years after Emancipation." *Washington Post*, June 19, 2019. www.washingtonpost.com/outlook/2019/06/19/why-racial-wealth-gap-persists-more-than-years-after-emancipation.

Schmidt, Samantha. "Americans' Views Flipped on Gay Rights. How Did Minds Change So Quickly?" *Washington Post*, June 7, 2019. www.washingtonpost.com/local/social-issues/americans-views-flipped-on-gay-rights-how-did-minds-change-so-quickly/2019/06/07/ae256016-8720-11e9-98c1-e945ae5db8fb_story.html.

Searcey, Dionne, John Eligon, and Farah Stockman. "After Protests, Politicians Reconsider Police Budgets and Discipline." *New York Times*, June 9, 2020. www.nytimes.com/2020/06/08/us/unrest-defund-police.html.

Sengupta, Somini. "Protesting Climate Change, Young People Take to Streets in a Global Strike." *New York Times*, Sept. 20, 2019. www.nytimes.com/2019/09/20/climate/global-climate-strike.html.

———. "Young New Yorkers Want You to Know Why They're Marching." *New York Times*, June 13, 2020. www.nytimes.com/2020/06/13/nyregion/nyc-protests-george-floyd.html.

Shapiro, Eliza. "Segregation Has Been the Story of New York City's Schools for 50 Years." *New York Times*, Mar. 26, 2019. www.nytimes.com/2019/03/26/nyregion/school-segregation-new-york.html.

Smith, David. "DeRay Mckesson on Black Lives Matter: 'It Changed the Country.'" *Guardian*, Dec. 30, 2019. www.theguardian.com/us-news/2019/dec/30/deray-mckesson-black-lives-matter-interview.

Smith, Nikkolas. "Nikkolas Smith: Art Can Help Show That Black Lives Matter. It Can Also Lead to Activism." *Time*, Aug. 20, 2020. time.com/5880948/nikkolas-smith-art-activism.

SNCC Digital Gateway, The Student Nonviolent Coordinating Committee Legacy Project. Duke University Libraries and the Center for Documentary Studies at Duke University. snccdigital.org.

Streeter, Kurt. "Kneeling, Fiercely Debated in the N.F.L., Resonates in Protests." *New York Times*, June 5, 2020. www.nytimes.com/2020/06/05/sports/football/george-floyd-kaepernick-kneeling-nfl-protests.html.

———. "Maya Moore Left Basketball. A Prisoner Needed Her Help." *New York Times*, June 30, 2019. www.nytimes.com/2019/06/30/sports/maya-moore-wnba-quit.html.

Sugrue, Thomas J. "2020 Is Not 1968: To Understand Today's Protests, You Must Look Further Back." *National Geographic*, June 11, 2020. www.nationalgeographic.com/history/2020/06/2020-not-1968.

Tavernise, Sabrina, and John Eligon. "Voters Say Black Lives Matter Protests Were Important. They Disagree

on Why." *New York Times*, Nov. 7, 2020. www.nytimes.com/2020/11/07/us/black-lives-matter-protests.html.

Taylor, Derrick Bryson. "George Floyd Protests: A Timeline." *New York Times*, Jan. 6, 2021. www.nytimes.com/article/george-floyd-protests-timeline.html.

Taylor, Keeanga-Yamahtta. "The Players' Revolt Against Racism, Inequality, and Police Terror." *New Yorker*, Sept. 9, 2020. www.newyorker.com/news/our-columnists/the-players-revolt-against-racism-inequality-and-police-terror.

Tesler, Michael. "Support for Black Lives Matter Surged during Protests, but Is Waning among White Americans." *FiveThirtyEight*, Aug. 19, 2020. fivethirtyeight.com/features/support-for-black-lives-matter-surged-during-protests-but-is-waning-among-white-americans.

Vanity Fair. "Black Lives Matter Co-Founder Alicia Garza Breaks Down Her Career." Sept. 11, 2020. Video, 24:54. www.vanityfair.com/video/watch/careert-timeline-black-lives-matter-co-founder-breaks-down-her-career.

Vitale, Alex S. *The End of Policing*. New York: Verso, 2017.

Williams, Timothy, and John Eligon. "The Lives of Ferguson Activists, Five Years Later." *New York Times*, Aug. 9, 2019. www.nytimes.com/2019/08/09/us/ferguson-activists.html.

Wilson, Christopher. "Lessons Worth Learning from the Moment Four Students Sat Down to Take a Stand." *Smithsonian Magazine*, Jan. 31, 2020. www.smithsonianmag.com/smithsonian-institution/lessons-worth-learning-moment-greensboro-four-sat-down-lunch-counter-180974087.

Wortham, Jenna. "A 'Glorious Poetic Rage.'" *New York Times*, June 5, 2020. www.nytimes.com/2020/06/05/sunday-review/black-lives-matter-protests-floyd.html.

———. "How a New Wave of Black Activists Changed the Conversation." *New York Times*, Aug. 25, 2020. www.nytimes.com/2020/08/25/magazine/black-visions-collective.html.

Yee, Vivian. "'I Can't Breathe' Is Echoed in Voices of Fury and Despair." *New York Times*, Dec. 4, 2014. www.nytimes.com/2014/12/04/nyregion/i-cant-breathe-is-re-echoed-in-voices-of-fury-and-despair.html.

Zaveri, Mihir. "'I Need People to Hear My Voice': Teens Protest Racism." *New York Times*, June 23, 2020. www.nytimes.com/2020/06/23/us/teens-protest-black-lives-matter.html.

INDEX

Page numbers in italics refer to photographs.